# I WAS
# JACK
# MORTIMER

'Very few novels published in recent
years match its daunting panache...
A truly clever, rather wonderful book that
both plays with and defies genre'
IRISH TIMES

'The cast of this brilliant thriller... are pure
Raymond Chandler... but the Viennese
setting gives it an extra, stylish twist. It's
excellently written and fearsomely gripping'
THE TIMES

'A fascinating snapshot of Vienna between
the wars, pacey and entertaining'
GUARDIAN

ALEXANDER LERNET-HOLENIA (1897–1976) was born in Vienna. He served in the Austro-Hungarian army in the First World War and became a protégé of Rainer Maria Rilke. During his life he wrote poetry, novels, plays and was a successful screenwriter. His uneasy relationship with the National Socialist Party resulted in his removal from prominence in 1944, but after the end of the Second World War, he again became a vital figure in Austrian cultural life.

IGNAT AVSEY was a distinguished translator from Russian and German. His published translations include Dostoevsky's *The Karamazov Brothers*, *The Idiot*, *The Village of Stepanchikovo* and *Humiliated and Insulted*.

# I WAS
# JACK
# MORTIMER

## ALEXANDER
## LERNET-HOLENIA

TRANSLATED FROM THE GERMAN
BY IGNAT AVSEY

PUSHKIN PRESS CLASSICS

Pushkin Press
Somerset House, Strand
London WC2R 1LA

*I Was Jack Mortimer* was first published in German
as *Ich war Jack Mortimer* in 1933

First published by Pushkin Press in 2013
This edition published 2024

1 3 5 7 9 8 6 4 2

ISBN 13: 978-1-80533-037-0

Designed and typeset by Tetragon, London
Printed and bound in the United Kingdom by Clays Ltd, Elcograf S.p.A.

www.pushkinpress.com

# I WAS
# JACK
# MORTIMER

# 1

U P ON THE HILLTOP MARKET, behind a row of cabs parked nose to tail, stood a small group of drivers, chatting and smoking cigarettes.

Flocks of pink-footed, iridescent grey-and-white pigeons pecked at the rubbish between the stalls of the steeply cobbled square, or from time to time took off and glided high above before settling on the house gables, in particular on a pink-washed palace, where most of them nested.

The sky was overcast. The rows of windows shone like burnished silver. The air was heavy with the smell of vegetables, flowers and fruit.

It was a mild November day.

Two cabs with passengers pulled out in close succession from the left of the rank and out of the square, and someone was already calling out the name of the next driver, who, with his coat undone and his elbows resting on the balustrade of the nearby memorial, was chatting to his mates.

He was a young man of about thirty with dark-blue eyes beneath brown eyebrows.

Hearing his name, he took a quick drag at his cigarette,

chucked it away and, buttoning up his coat at the same time, hurried to his cab.

A woman in a dark, bold-striped suit, a fox fur slung over her shoulder, was just about to get in. She had already delicately poised one foot on the running board; she held an open handbag in her gloved left hand, and was looking at herself in the mirror as she adjusted her hair under her hat with her other, ungloved hand.

She couldn't have been more than twenty, smartly dressed, even if with that slight nonchalance which is so irresistible in young women.

With her little finger she now wiped a spot of excess lipstick from her lips, and was examining her mouth carefully as the driver approached her. He caught a glimpse of her face in the mirror as he stood behind her. A pair of large grey eyes gazed at him from under a short veil as she tilted the mirror to see who was there.

The driver bowed, stepped back and opened the door.

"Sixty-two Prinz-Eugen-Strasse," she said without turning, and, snapping her handbag shut, stuck it under her arm and got into the cab.

He closed the door. Two of the other drivers made a sign to him as he was settling behind the wheel. He looked at them quizzically and turned on the ignition.

"Not bad, eh?" they indicated.

"What?" he queried, as though he hadn't understood.

The two pointed inside the car.

He mumbled something and waited till the road was clear. He had hardly pulled out when he felt himself blushing. The two drivers, who'd noticed his embarrassment, grinned.

He changed up and drew his hand across his forehead.

He was now in the thick of the traffic.

Nevertheless, he suddenly threw his head back, but couldn't see the girl in the rear because of the glare from the glass partition.

After a few moments he reached for the rear-view mirror and adjusted it slowly till he saw her.

She was sitting, legs crossed, holding her handbag and looking out of the window.

He had to stop at the next junction. He sat and stared into the mirror while the car was stationary. And even when the traffic was moving again, he continued looking into the rear through the mirror.

As a result he almost collided in Kärntner Strasse with a car that had turned out of a side street. He managed to brake with a violent jolt at the last moment, and the offended driver, shaking his head, swung out in front of him. He followed him closely till the car pulled up just before the Opera, to which he again failed to react, and before it had come to a halt he hit it, inching it forward with his bumper.

The driver turned round, swearing loudly as he got out, and ran to the back to see what the damage was, while the policeman who was standing at the junction also approached when he saw what had happened.

9

"The fellow's clueless," the man yelled, grasping the petrol tank of his car. "He nearly ran into me a moment ago!"

"What's your name?" the policeman asked.

"Ferdinand Sponer," the young man answered apologetically. However, since no damage had been done, the policeman waved them on. "Be more careful in future," he said, and walked back to his post, while the other driver, swearing profusely, got back in his car. Sponer, however, turned round to his glamorous passenger, "I'm awfully sorry!"

"Why," she said from the back of the car, "didn't you take Seilerstätte if you don't know how to drive?"

Seilerstätte is a quiet street, parallel to Kärntner Strasse, with little traffic.

"Oh, but I do," he mumbled, and smiled sheepishly.

"Move on!" the policeman shouted. The car in front had in the meantime driven off. Other cars were piling up behind Sponer. He hastily pulled out and joined the traffic. He turned left at the Opera into Mahlerstrasse, behind the Grand Hotel, then right, crossed the ring road, and, accelerating, cut across the Schwartzenbergplatz and sped up Prinz-Eugen-Strasse. At number sixty-two he did a U-turn, pointing towards the centre again, and stopped in front of the house.

"My apologies once again," he said as his attractive fare alighted. She paid, glanced at him and shook her head. He tried to smile once more. She turned away and walked towards the main entrance. With a wonderfully graceful movement she swung open a small side gate mounted in the main entrance and stepped inside.

He followed her with his eyes until the gate fell shut behind her. Then he stared at the entrance.

A few minutes later he noticed he was still holding the money she had given him.

He started the car but drove on just a few yards, stopped again and got out. After standing hesitantly by the car a few seconds, he walked up to the main entrance and went in.

In the high, timber-panelled entrance hall, at the far end of which, through a French window, he glimpsed an overgrown garden, he noticed the porter's lodge on the right and the open door to the stairwell on the left.

A huge, gilt chandelier hung from the decorated ceiling, and short flights of steps led off from the right and left of the entrance hall.

He stepped into the stairwell and glanced up at the high, wide lift shaft with the staircase snaking around it. He couldn't hear any footsteps on the stairs or the landings.

On the wall hung a black, polished, framed board with white, numbered bell-buttons. Under each was a card bearing the name of the respective occupant.

He struck a match in order to read the names, as it had already turned dark. The residents included army officers, civil servants, aristocrats, as well as an industrialist.

He tried to picture which of them could have a daughter like the beautiful young girl he'd driven here; or on which of them a girl, just like the one in a dark-green suit with a fox slung over her shoulders, might have dropped in; or which of them a young woman, smartly dressed, even if with a slight, though irresistible, touch of nonchalance, might be paying a visit.

However, the names revealed nothing.

They didn't reveal which apartment she'd entered, or what she was doing there, whether she was sitting with her parents, or with friends, having tea, or with her lover, whom even now she was embracing and kissing.

The match went out and burnt his finger. He let go of it, crushed it with his foot, and found himself in semi-darkness.

Finally he left the stairwell, stood hesitatingly for a moment in front of the porter's lodge, and entered. He opened the glass door, stepped into the lobby, and knocked at the door to the porter's flat. A couple of steps led down into a sort of combined kitchen and living room.

A child was playing in the middle of the floor; next to the door, at a table covered with a blue-patterned oilcloth, sat a woman of about forty-five with the light on, doing what such people always do in their flats—sitting with the light on, of course, drinking coffee, reading the paper, and thinking about family matters.

She glanced up as Sponer entered.

"Did a young woman come in about five minutes ago?" he asked. And, when she continued looking at him, he added, "In a green suit with a fox fur."

"Why?" the woman asked, dunked a piece of roll in her coffee and continued reading the paper.

"I've a letter for her."

The woman put out her hand.

"To be delivered personally," he said.

"Second floor, on the right, Countess Dünewald," and she stuck the piece of roll in her mouth and turned over the page.

Well, well, he thought, a Countess! Probably the daughter. And, as he glanced from the porter's wife to the newspaper with artist's sketches illustrating some crime reports, he said: "No, not the…"

"Not the what?" the woman asked.

"Not the Countess." He rummaged in his pockets and pulled out a letter. He pretended he was looking at the address.

"Her niece?" the woman asked.

"Yes," he said, and then almost without thinking, "the Duchess."

"She's no duchess."

"Isn't she? Ah," he went on, "you're right, it doesn't say that here either. But, anyway, it's her niece."

"Let me see," she said, and held out her hand once again for the letter.

"No, I just wanted to check that the names tallied."

"Raschitz?"

"That's the one," he said, as if simply confirming the fact. "And the first name?"

13

She again wanted to see the letter.

He stuck it back in his pocket. "No, that's all right," he said. He didn't find out the first name. "Second floor, on the right, then?" he said. "Thanks." And he adjusted his cap and left. He noticed she was staring at him as he closed the door. She had become curious and went to the door of the flat. He therefore pretended he was going to deliver the letter. He walked to the stairwell, mounted a couple of steps and stopped. It occurred to him that he really could walk up. He ascended a few more steps. On the second floor, on the right-hand door he saw a brass plate with the name "Dünewald".

He waited two or three minutes and then walked down the stairs again. When he came to the entrance hall he saw that the woman was still standing at the door, staring. He got into his car and waited.

Every now and again trams passed up and down Prinz-Eugen-Strasse, and a couple of cars raced past.

Dry leaves from the Schwarzenberg Park fluttered in the wind.

He told a couple of people who wanted to get in that he'd been hired already.

He waited till about half past seven.

It had gone dark long ago; a strong wind had got up, and the street lamps flickered and swayed.

The porter's wife came out of the house once, but he turned his face away and she didn't recognize him.

At about half past seven the girl appeared, accompanied

14

by two handsome older men, dressed in the manner of ex-cavalry officers. The three took no notice of the cab. They walked past, chatting about bridge.

They walked down the street. Sponer drove slowly behind them. After a while they turned left into a side street, then right into Alleegasse. They stopped in front of number sixteen. The two gentlemen said goodbye. The girl went into the house, and the men walked off in the direction of the centre of the town.

During that evening and the next morning, Sponer found out from the doormen in Alleegasse and from the head waiter of the nearby Café Attaché, but in particular from a commissionaire who used to sit either on the street corner or in a bar opposite, under a sign with two white horses, that the girl was called Marisabelle von Raschitz, that she was the daughter of a major, and was indeed the niece of Countess Dünewald, the widow of Count Dünewald, the erstwhile household steward of Archduchess Maria Isabella, after whom the young lady, whom the commissionaire had known since childhood, had been duly christened.

"They say," he added, "that Major von Raschitz is still a wealthy man. Marisabelle also has a brother." The commissionaire knew him, too, from childhood. He said that he'd often chatted to the two lovely young children when they were taken for walks. In Vienna, children, even from the upper classes would, in former times, happily talk to servant girls on street corners or to elderly invalids in the Belvedere Gardens. These invalids had either lost an arm or had a peg leg, they wore uniforms of days gone by, looked after the park amenities and used to talk to the children and their nannies; the commissionaire also reminisced about former times, about the Archduchess, her household, and the splendid carriages with their gilt wheels. Sponer listened to him for a while, nodded absentmindedly, and got back in his car.

In the next side street there was a taxi rank. He parked his cab there, got out and walked to the corner, from where he could observe the house. However, when the cabs that were parked in front had picked up fares and it was his turn, he explained, after driving a few yards, that there was something wrong with his car, and he let the others take his place. Some of the drivers offered to help. Sponer declined. He started tinkering with the engine himself.

At about eleven he saw Marisabelle leave the house. She wore a brown skirt and a short fur jacket. Her long gloves were still under her arm, but she started to put them on as she headed towards the centre.

Immediately afterwards, the house gates opened and a Cadillac drove out. Two men were sitting in the back. The Cadillac turned into the side street in which Sponer was tinkering with his engine.

He stopped, walked up to the commissionaire, and asked him whose car it was.

"It belongs to an industrialist," the commissionaire replied. A certain Herr So-and-so, who also lived in the same building. Sponer didn't register the name. But he asked if the Raschitzes, too, owned a car. The commissionaire replied in the affirmative.

Sponer now picked up a fare, then a second one at the Church of the Nine Choirs of Angels, who had to make several business calls at various government offices and departments, and for whom Sponer had to wait at each stop. When, however, at about one o'clock in Schwarzspanierstrasse there still appeared to be no end to these calls, Sponer asked his fare to leave, since he had come to the end of his shift. He drove back at breakneck speed to Alleegasse, and parked to await Marisabelle's return.

She didn't return, however, and at about two he reluctantly concluded that he had probably missed her. In the café Zu den Zwei Schimmeln he had a bite to eat with the commissionaire, who also had a few beers and regaled him and the other clients with tales of the former imperial court. In Vienna there were still quite a few of these old commissionaires, minor officials, former servants and the like, who sported side whiskers and waxed nostalgically about the Court, the Arcièren Life Guards, the huge tips dispensed by the foreign potentates, the Emperor's house guests, and much more besides. Sponer, who was twenty-nine and knew hardly anything about such things, listened without paying much attention, constantly glancing over the street to the windows with the curtains.

I shall, he thought, park in front of the house so that when she comes out in the afternoon I can ask if she wants a cab.

He paid, left, and drove to Alleegasse. He stopped in front of the main entrance, pointing towards the city centre. After a short while a policeman asked him what he was doing there parked for so long. "I'm picking up a fare," Sponer replied. "He hasn't come down yet, he's still in the house."

The commissionaire, who by now was becoming suspicious of Sponer's behaviour, also came over and asked him a question, which, however, Sponer completely ignored. For at this very moment Marisabelle emerged from the house. She was wearing a dark coat and a two-tone hat.

Sponer sprang from his seat and approached her.

"A cab?" he asked.

She shook her head and was about to continue on her way, when she recognized him.

"Ah!" she said, and since he was standing so close to her, "It's you, is it?" But she didn't stop and kept walking.

"Yes, it's me," he said, and, searching for words, tried to stand in her way. "Would… would you like me to give you a lift? I was so upset yesterday about that little incident. My driving's really quite good…"

She looked at him. A shadow of a smile flitted across her mouth. A row of dazzlingly white teeth flashed for a brief second.

"I'm glad!" she said. "How long have you been a driver then?"

"Four years. Do you drive yourself?"

"Me?" she asked in surprise.

"Yes."

"A little," she said.

"I had an idea you would have a car. Of course," he added immediately, "I learnt to drive somewhere else… with my relatives, you understand." And he paused for a split second. She looked at him as though she couldn't quite fathom why he had said "you understand". And it must have crossed her mind: "What relatives? What on earth have they got to do with it?"

"When I first started," he continued immediately, "I'd far rather have done something else than be a driver…"

"Really?" she said, and made as if to walk on again.

"Yes," he said hastily, "I even spent a whole year in… a cadet school… Actually, my father was…"

It seemed she couldn't care less that he had been a cadet. "Yes," she said, "nowadays all sorts become drivers. That's the way it is… one just has to…"

He tried to smile. She looked away, but then turned towards him again. He was above average height, well built, only his hands were rough. As she looked at his face, she noticed he had beautiful eyes.

She blushed slightly, nodded curtly, and turned away.

"So, no car?" he asked.

"No, thank you," she said quickly, and walked on.

He stared after her.

2

H<small>E FINISHED HIS SHIFT AT SIX.</small> He didn't take the car home, however, but gave it, together with the day's takings, to the other driver, Georg Haintl, in Margaretenstrasse. Then he caught a tram to Fünfhaus, one of the outer suburbs, where he rented a room from Herr Oxenbauer, a railwayman, near the garage where he kept his cab.

Without taking off his coat, he sat down on his bed and leant against the shabby old wall-hanging depicting a lurcher giving chase to a hare.

The smell of petrol wafted from the adjacent room; the door to it, blocked by a washstand, was shut.

He got up and flung the window open.

On the far side of a backyard, which was bordered only by a low wall, rows of street lights flickered around the perimeter of a large undeveloped plot of land. In the darkness of an adjoining garden, shrubbery rustled in the wind. He pulled off his coat, threw himself on the bed and lit a cigarette.

Shortly afterwards, the railwayman's teenage daughter brought him his supper on a black tray with a faded golden pattern. She was about to put it on his bedside table, but he motioned with his head to the other table.

"Why does it smell of petrol?"

"I can't smell anything," she said.

"I should have known!" he turned on her. "Every time there's a smell, I'm told there's no smell at all, every time the soup's off, I'm told it's not off at all, and so on!"

She went out, slamming the door. He followed her with his eyes from under closely knit brows.

She didn't like him because she couldn't stand Marie Fiala.

Marie Fiala was his girlfriend.

She arrived about ten minutes later. When she entered, he was still lying on his bed and hadn't eaten anything.

She kissed him and asked why he hadn't touched his food. Wasn't he hungry? They'd be late for the film. Unless, of course, he didn't want to go. In which case there was no need to go out at all. She didn't really mind. And she sat down in her coat, next to him.

"I don't really feel like going anywhere," he said.

She nodded, got up and took her coat off. In the meantime he went over to the table and ate a few mouthfuls. She joined him at the table. She wasn't pretty, but had a good figure and marvellous blonde hair, which now shimmered in the light of the lamp.

"Would you like me to sort out some of your things?" she asked.

"That'd be nice," he mumbled, picking up the tray with

the uneaten food and putting it outside the door. "Have you eaten already?" he asked, when he was back in the room.

"Yes," she said. She had opened the wardrobe, taken out a few of his underclothes, and was holding them up to the light.

"We can always go to the cinema later," he said.

"I'm easy either way," she replied.

She took her handbag and rummaged in it for a needle and thread. He offered her a cigarette, which she stuck between her lips before getting down to work.

He shut the window, sat down on the bed, leant on his elbows and looked at her. The light played on her hair.

They were planning to get married, but kept putting it off for various reasons: if the truth be known, only because they'd already known each other for too long. In the meantime she'd lost her job as a shop assistant, had then been unemployed for months at a stretch, and was now helping out here and there at a friend's, taking in washing and doing mending and stitching jobs.

She still hoped, of course, that he'd marry her, only she never mentioned it.

He watched her all the while she was working, and sometimes made a comment or two. She asked him where he'd been all day, and he in turn asked her what she'd been doing.

Every now and then, she returned the inspected items to the wardrobe and brought new ones to the table.

Finally she put her needle away. He kissed her hands, drew

her to him and kissed her on the lips. Then they stroked each other's cheeks.

They remained like that for some time and listened to the wind blowing round the house. And they thought how long they had already known each another. Or rather, they didn't think, they simply felt how unhappy they were.

At about nine they went to the cinema after all.

Then he took her home.


He didn't have to go to work till midday the next day.

At about nine he took the tram to the centre.

In Alleegasse he didn't see the commissionaire, who was probably on an errand. He was therefore able to walk up and down in front of Marisabelle's house without having to engage in tedious conversation.

It was a sunny autumn day. At the top of the street, where it climbed slightly, the wind blew dead foliage from the Theresianum Gardens. The tall windows of the palace reflected the sky above.

Sponer stopped at a Packard that was parked in front of one of the houses.

The chauffeur started talking to him, but almost immediately the owner of the car appeared, and they drove off.

At about eleven Marisabelle came out of the entrance. She was again wearing the same grey suit and a fox over her shoulders.

Sponer went up to her straight away, before she had even closed the gate, and his heart began to pound.

"Excuse me," he said, "for troubling you yesterday, I only wanted… I'm…"

She looked at him while the gate swung shut.

"I don't have my car today," he continued quickly. "I only wanted to apologize."

She didn't reply immediately. "What for?" she asked, finally.

"About yesterday," he said. "I didn't want you to think that I was trying to force you into anything."

"Really," she said, and it seemed as though she wanted to say something else.

"But I'd have had no other opportunity of speaking to you…"

"You wanted to speak to me?"

"Yes," he said, and looked down.

She leant against the gate and smiled, although he didn't notice it. But when he looked up again, she merely said, "What about?"

"I just wanted," he said after a pause, "to… just to see you…"

She took her handbag, which was under her left arm, transferred it to the other arm, fiddled for a moment with the fingers of her glove, and then looked up at Sponer again.

"But," he said, "you walked away so quickly… I quite understand you were annoyed that I spoke to you yesterday,

I do apologize, but otherwise I wouldn't have had any opportunity to…"

She watched him while he spoke, and also, after he broke off, she kept looking into his face; finally, she lowered her eyes. "Look here," she said, pulling her gloves on, "you really shouldn't be talking to me like this here."

"Would you," he said, "at least allow me to…"

She remained silent.

"…accompany you for a short distance?"

"No," she said. She stood there for a moment, drew the fox round her shoulders, and strode off.

He took two or three steps after her, stopped and glanced around. No one appeared to have noticed them. He took another couple of steps, hesitated, and then followed Marisabelle at a distance of about thirty yards.

She walked in the direction of the centre, without turning round once. At the next side street she stopped for a moment and then crossed the street. She reached up to her shoulder once and adjusted her fur. She acknowledged the greetings of a man whom she passed near Karlskirche. Her gait was carefree and relaxed, as if unconcerned whether anyone was following her or not.

Sponer caught up with her at Karlsplatz Gardens.

She neither appeared surprised, nor gave any indication that she suspected he had been following her. But she stopped at the edge of the gardens, where the leaves were falling. A couple of large crows pecked about on the grass. She placed one foot on the base of a low trellis that bordered the grass, opened her handbag, looked in the mirror and pulled her short veil farther down. Then she let her handbag slide down, and looked at him.

His eyebrows were drawn tight. "You know," he said, "what I'm going to say to you, don't you?"

She lifted the mirror once more and looked at her mouth. "And what do you expect me to answer?" she asked.

He remained silent.

She wiped some powder from her cheek. Then she snapped her handbag shut. "Well?" she said.

He shrugged his shoulders.

"You're a strange person," she said.

"Why?" he asked in astonishment.

She looked at him. She nearly said, "Because you've such beautiful eyes," but instead she only said, "Because to start with, you accost me, and then you just stand there and expect me to carry on talking. Is that what you always do?"

He blushed. "No," he said.

Every woman wants to have an affair with a man who finds her attractive.

"You wouldn't even have spoken to me otherwise."

He hesitated for a second. "I've fallen in love with you," he said.

She looked at the lawn, where the leaves were falling. "You just can't say a thing like that," she said. "All right, you can say a few words to me, but you can't suddenly say you love me. You don't even know me."

"I know, of course, who you are," he said.

She looked hard at him.

"You've been making enquiries about me?" she asked.

"Yes."

So, he'd been making enquiries about her, had he? She had got in his cab, he'd driven her just that once, fallen in love with her, tried to find out who she was, waited in front of her house either in his cab, when on duty, or without his cab, when off duty. He had fallen in love with her. He had beautiful eyes. She'd spoken a few words to him. He was a handsome man, a driver. That was all there was to it.

She thrust her handbag under her arm.

"Listen," she said, "please go now. You've told me that you like me, but you don't have to fall in love with everyone you like. Perhaps you don't even realize yourself that we don't have anything in common. We can't just stand here any longer like this. Someone passing may see us. You'd better go now."

He didn't finish work till about eight. Then he telephoned Marie Fiala at her neighbour's, who had a phone; after that, they met in a small coffee house out in the suburbs.

They had often met there before, and would sit happily for hours on end, even if sometimes they didn't say a word to each other, but just sat there and smoked. As usual, there were a few people sitting at the tables and on the red benches along the wall, reading newspapers; waiters rested their trays on the counter for an instant; the cashier dispensed lumps of sugar; and the waiters carried on serving. The lamps were enveloped in a fine haze of cigarette smoke; the fan hummed for a bit and then went dead; everything was still again.

Later, however, the silence was interrupted when she remarked that he wasn't talking. They knew each other too well. She loved him, of course, and had no end of things to say, but one can't carry on talking if the other person is unwilling to speak. For his part, he loved her after a fashion. She was there and he simply took her for granted. He'd had a few fleeting affairs on the side, but had broken them off every time, and always returned to her just because she was there. She hadn't even noticed anything—at least that's what he thought.

By the time he had entered the coffee house, she still hadn't arrived. He had sat down on one of the benches and stared in front of him. She arrived a few minutes later. He stood up and helped her out of her coat. They then chatted, and though the conversation dragged rather, they still continued talking. The waiter placed a couple of newspapers on the table. Sponer picked one up and, answering her every so often, leafed desultorily through the paper.

After some time he realized that Marie was no longer speaking. He looked at her and saw tears in her eyes.

28

She wiped them away hastily.

"What's the matter?" he asked.

"Nothing," she said, and forced herself to smile.

"Are you all right?" he asked.

She merely shook her head.

"Shall we leave?" he asked after a pause.

"No," she said. "Unless you'd rather…"

He asked for the bill.

They left the premises, but instead of going back to his room, he took her home. They didn't have far to go, just a couple of hundred yards. They'd been going out for years; now it was just a couple of minutes' walk together.

At the main entrance they kissed each other, and she suddenly let her head fall on his shoulder.

He stroked her hair. Then she opened the front gate and went in.

It was the end of a love affair that just would not end.


The next day he was on duty again. At about eleven he drove to Alleegasse, parked the cab in the side street, next to the other cabs, and walked to the corner.

The commissionaire was there as usual and struck up a conversation with Sponer, but since the latter answered only in monosyllables, he left him and strode over to the other drivers. At half past eleven Marisabelle appeared. She must have reckoned that Sponer would be there, for she glanced round, saw him and remained standing at the main entrance.

He walked straight up to her.

"I'm sorry," he said hastily, "to bother you again… but my car's over there, otherwise I'd have waited for you farther down. I…"

She looked at him inquiringly.

"What do you want?"

"I wanted you to… I only wanted to say a few words to you…"

She took hold of the door handle. "I told you already that you're not to speak to me."

"Y-yes," he stuttered, "not here. But I just wanted to ask if you… seeing as my car's here…" He fell silent and looked at her.

Her lips trembled. "Leave me alone," she said.

"Please listen!" he begged.

"No, go away," she said, and pushed the gate open with her shoulder.

"Please, don't go," he pleaded.

"No, leave me alone!" she shouted, and stepped back.

He took a step forwards as though to stop her, but she slipped through the gate and slammed it shut in front of him.

For a brief moment he was about to follow her, but turned round and went over to his cab. The other drivers looked on, but pretended that nothing had happened. He got in and sat motionless for a second, then he turned the engine on, swung sharply out of the rank, and sped off.

He had to speak to her. She had got it all wrong. It wasn't a case of someone simply chatting up a girl in the street!

After he'd calmed down a bit, he drove various fares till about half past three, then parked again in Alleegasse itself, rather than in the side street.

The drivers who were now standing on the corner were different to the ones who were there in the morning.

He waited till after six, but with no luck.

The commissionaire kept looking across, then got up and took a couple of steps towards him to strike up a conversation, but turned back, for he now found the whole thing rather odd; and besides, Sponer was giving him strange looks. He retraced his steps to his usual spot on the street corner, which he soon vacated, however, and went into the hotel.

He could keep a lookout from there.

After six, by which time it had already got dark, Marisabelle finally came out of the house. Sponer got out immediately.

She was followed closely by a young man of about eighteen, who closed the gate. Marisabelle stopped as soon as she caught sight of Sponer. When her companion drew level with her, she said something to him quickly in a soft voice. The young man raised his head, and went straight over to Sponer.

"Will you stop pestering my sister?" he said in a loud, clear voice, standing straight in front of him. "Is that understood? Clear out of here, or else! If I see you in front of this house once more, you'll have only yourself to blame for the consequences!"

He turned round, took Marisabelle by the arm, and they walked off in the other direction.

Sponer stood rooted to the ground, then took a step forward to go after the young man and box his ears, but he restrained himself and got back into his cab.

Barely controlling his anger, he turned on the engine, screeched round the next corner and sped up the side street. At the crossing with Favoritenstrasse he slowed down, but, fuming with rage and finding himself in a maze of back streets, with no idea where he was going, he decided to head for one of the railway stations. It was beginning to rain; he raced though the city, with its brightly lit windows and cars glistening in the wet, towards the Westbahnhof. Spray thrown up by the wind blew across his path. His cheeks were burning. He pulled off a glove and wiped his face with his bare hand.

As he turned into the station approach, he nearly ran over a dog, which jumped back, barking at him.

A lot of cabs were already lined up in rows at the arrivals exit. He backed into an empty space, switched off the engine and stared straight ahead.

After a few minutes there was some movement among the parked cabs. He glanced at his watch. The Paris–Munich express had probably just pulled in. People were streaming out of the exit. The cabs edged forward, picking up fares and luggage, and disappeared in the direction of the centre. Finally it was Sponer's turn. One of the porters standing by the taxi rank picked up two suitcases, shoved one on the seat next to Sponer and the other in the back.

A man in an overcoat got in and said, "Hotel Bristol."

The porter slammed the door shut.

Sponer turned to the right out of the station, then left, drove between two dimly lit parks on either side, heard several loud explosions coming from the exhaust of a lorry he was overtaking, and emerged two turnings later at Mariahilfer Strasse. It was busy; there was a lot of traffic at this time of night. A couple of minutes later, he veered off to the right into a less well-lit street, which ran uphill, drove straight on in the direction of the city, crossed over Getreidemarkt, turned right into a residential district, then left again, and came out on the ring road, just in front of the Opera House. Reaching back with his left hand, he slid open the glass partition separating him from the back of the cab, and spoke over his shoulder.

"The Old or the New Bristol?"

As there was no answer, he said, as he joined the ring road, "There are two Bristols, the old and the new one. Which do you want?" While he was speaking, he turned off the main carriageway immediately in front of the Opera House, swung into the parallel slip road, and pulled up next to the front steps, since the lights at the Opera intersection were against him.

There was still no answer from the man in the back.

Sponer turned round and saw him leaning back in the right-hand corner, staring impassively out of the widow at Kärntner Strasse.

"Old or New Bristol, which one?" he repeated.

The man did not react in the slightest.

Sponer turned on the interior light and saw him leaning back heavily. His coat was undone and he was clutching his right side with both hands as though looking for something in his pocket. His head was slumped to one side and his mouth was half open.

He remained completely motionless.

The man was dead.

# 3

S PONER STARED, terror-stricken, not so much seeing as sensing in a flash what had happened. A wave of fear hit him like a blow to the body. He started, pushed the door open and, freeing his coat which had snagged on the steering wheel, staggered backwards onto the pavement, before tearing the back door open and leaning inside. He grabbed the dead man by the chest with both hands and shook him. His head, as though snapped at the neck, lolled this way and that, slumped forward under its own weight; the body sagged to the floor like a sack of potatoes between the seat and the suitcase, and the head then fell back again, the face turned up blankly to the roof of the cab. The mouth fell open, and a thin trickle of blood ran from one corner over his chin and behind his shirt collar.

As the head fell back it revealed a bullet hole in the man's throat; the tie and shirt collar were soaked in blood. There must have been another bullet in his chest, because after Sponer withdrew his hands his gloves were wet and sticky.

He edged backwards out of the cab, straightened up and struck his head hard against the top of the door frame. His cap fell forward over his face. He instinctively pushed it back with his forearm instead of with his blood-stained gloved hand. He turned round.

A couple of people who were walking past some distance away took no notice. A taxi with its lights on and the driver standing next to it does not arouse anyone's curiosity. Still dazed from the impact against the door frame, Sponer took two or three steps forward to attract someone's attention, but, as nobody took any notice, he turned around towards a small news stand on the edge of the pavement where, despite the rain, they were still selling papers. A man had just bought a couple of evening editions and, as Sponer approached, both he and the newspaper seller turned their backs on him. Sponer wanted to say something, but couldn't. His lips moved, but no sound issued. The man pulled out another paper from the rack and the seller passed him his change. Sponer, speechless that a dreadful thing had happened and no one seemed in the least concerned, stared at them. After a few moments he turned back to his cab as if in a trance.

He took a couple of slow steps, then three or four very quick ones. He pulled off his blood-stained gloves and threw them into the car. Closing his eyes momentarily, he slammed the rear door shut, then got in his seat, turned off the interior light and, closing his own door with his left hand, swung the car to the right and headed towards the policeman operating the traffic signals at the centre of the crossroads. Just at that moment, the lights turned green on the ring road. A stream of cars that had started moving again drove towards the crossing, but as Sponer cut across, all hell broke loose. Some drivers cursed and slammed on their brakes right in front of Sponer's car, others tried to swerve around him, while the majority pulled up behind with a jolt. The policeman yelled something. Sponer drove right up to him. "What the hell?" the policeman shouted. Sponer suddenly found himself front bumper to front bumper with a convertible that had been waiting in the right-hand lane at the crossing in order to join the ring road, and the driver, who was already moving, had to brake in the nick of time.

"Get back!" the policeman yelled, and pulled out his notebook from under the cuff of his sleeve to take down Sponer's number. Sponer leant out of the car window.

"Officer," he said, "I've…"

"Are you mad?" the policeman yelled.

"Officer!" Sponer called out. "I've got a…"

"Get back!" the policeman shouted.

Sponer went into reverse, but immediately collided with a car that was trying to negotiate round him. The policeman screamed at him.

"There's a dead man in my car!" Sponer shouted at the top of his voice, but the noise from the convertible which had braked in front of him and was now edging its way out of the jam drowned his words. The policeman raged and gesticulated; cars drove past. Sponer shouted to the policeman a few more times, but finally realized he couldn't get through to him, engaged first gear with a curse, swung round the policeman and, changing up rapidly, raced off in the direction of Kärntner Strasse.

He had to get to a police station. He turned left off Kärntner Strasse into Neuer Markt, sped along Plankengasse, and pulled up in front of the police station in Bräunerstrasse.

A policeman was standing at the door, but Sponer rushed past him. He had had enough of policemen; he was going to talk directly to the inspector. When he entered the charging room he saw three or four officers who were trying to restrain a drunk who had just been brought in.

Two of them were holding the man by his arms while a third tried to force him down on a bench. The drunk, however, was lashing out with his feet. Sponer turned to the fourth officer, who was barking out the orders.

"Something's happened," he said, but received no answer. He grabbed the officer's arm. "Inspector!" he said. The policeman turned towards him for a split second but was forced to turn round again because the drunk, having been briefly forced down onto the bench, had jumped up again and was about to break loose, whereupon all four officers hurled themselves at him. The drunk displayed extraordinary physical strength, as if the superior forces he was struggling against had driven him wild. In the end, however, the policemen overcame him by their sheer weight, and as he lay spluttering on the bench, they vented their anger in a torrent of abuse. Sponer stood in the middle of the room, and the events of the past minutes raced through his mind like short, randomly edited film clips:

the dead man, the speeding cars, the news stand, the dead man, the carriageway, the blood, the dead man, the streets, the dead man. Caught a taxi at the station. "Hotel Bristol!" Ten minutes' drive. "Old or New?" No reply. "There are two: the Old Bristol and the New." No answer. Light on. The man sitting there, not moving. Leaves his seat, starts shaking him. He slumps forward, the head lolls back. Blood from his mouth. He's wedged between the suitcase and the seat. Someone's shot him through the throat. Who? He was in the cab by himself! "Who?" asks the inspector. "The dead man!"—"And the other one?"—"What other one?"—"The one who shot him!"—"There wasn't anyone else."—"There must've been a second person who'd…"—"No, he was on his own."—"Where was the person who shot him then?"—"I don't know."—"But when you heard the shots and turned around…"—"I didn't hear any shots."—"You didn't hear any shots?"—"No. I mean, yes: it was probably some exhaust backfiring…"—"What type of backfiring?"—"A lorry I was overtaking."—"And when you turned around?"—"I didn't turn around."—"You didn't turn around?"—"No."— "Dammit, man!" the inspector yells. "Someone gets shot in your car, and you don't so much as turn around?"—"No, I thought…"—"A murder is committed in your car as you drive along, and you don't notice a thing? A man is bumped off so close behind you that you could reach out with your hand and touch him, and yet you see nothing, absolutely nothing of the murderer? You continue driving with the dead man in your car and expect me to believe you had no idea he was dead, and it was only after you touched him that he slumped forward, and is now lying between the seat and the suitcase, and the car's outside the door…"

"What do you want?"

The policemen had overpowered the drunk at last, and the officer whose arm Sponer had pulled now stood facing him and said, "What do you want?"

Sponer stared at him. He must've committed suicide. The man shot himself. That's right! Seeing as there wasn't anybody else there… On the other hand, if it wasn't suicide… If the dead man didn't even have a weapon on him… He hadn't seen one lying there. If, however, someone had jumped on the running board, pulled the door open, fired, slammed the door shut and jumped off… And you didn't notice a thing? Didn't hear the shots? Thought it was backfiring? And the man in the car didn't shout out when the other person burst in and attacked him? A person who'd just arrived is attacked and murdered before he even reaches his hotel… Why? Why on earth should anyone… I haven't got a clue who the murdered person was or who did it! How the hell should I know why the bastards did it in my car… the bastards, for that's what they are…

"Well?" the policeman asked. "What's the matter?"

"I…" Sponer said.

"Yes?"

"I… I only wanted to…"

"What did you want?"

"I wanted to see if a…"

"If a what?"

"If a mate of mine…"

"Yes?"

"If he's here," Sponer gasped.

"What mate?" the policeman asked.

"Another… another driver."

"Should he be here?"

"Yes."

"Why?"

"Because," Sponer stuttered, "because he… was involved in an accident."

"Oh? Do you have any details."

"I beg your pardon?"

"Where did the accident take place?"

"In town."

"Yes, but where?"

"On the Freyung."

"I see. Who else was involved?"

"It… it was a car."

"What type of car?"

"Another car."

The policeman frowned.

"Really?" he cried, clearly still furious after the struggle with the drunk. "Another car? Not his own? Are you trying to be funny?"

"No, Inspector," Sponer mumbled, "I only wanted to say…"

"What did you want to say?"

"I only wanted to ask if he was here."

"Who?" the policeman yelled. "What's his name?"

Let's get out of here, Sponer thought. Quick, before I start saying things that aren't true, otherwise they'll keep me here, and in the car they'll find the… "No, Inspector," he mumbled, "he's not here yet, but he's sure to…"

"What's his name?" the policeman bellowed.

"Georg… Georg Haintl," Sponer mumbled.

"Right!" The policeman grabbed a notepad. "And his registration number?"

Sponer was spared the need to answer. Just at that moment the drunk, having shaken off the three men who were holding him down, noiselessly and unexpectedly leapt to his feet and launched himself with all his force in a flying tackle from the back, straight at the knees of the policeman who was questioning Sponer. The officer fell down with a crash, but was instantly back on his feet with a cry of rage, and the four again pounced on the drunk. Sponer turned on his heel and ran out.

The policeman was still standing outside the main door. He hadn't a clue that there was a dead man in the car just three paces away from him. Sponer jumped into his seat and sped off.

For about ten minutes he raced aimlessly though the streets, then he came to his senses and looked round. He was in the ninth district, not far from the Liechtenstein Palace. He turned

42

off the meter without thinking. The person for whom he'd turned it on wouldn't be paying for the journey now.

He drove on and tried to recall the events. He found it impossible to gather his thoughts. It was as if there were an empty space, a blank between his brain and his thoughts. He couldn't concentrate on what he wanted to think about, because all kinds of unrelated matter kept racing through his head like mad. The moment he tried to think what he should do next, all kinds of thoughts tumbled through his head, except the one he wanted to focus on. As clearly as a maniac sees visions, he kept on seeing one of the two men get into the cab at the station, followed immediately by the other man jumping onto the running board from the other side and opening the door as the cab drove off. The two men were now screaming at each other, but he couldn't hear this due to the noise of the traffic, and then came the shots drowned by the noise of the confounded lorry and sounding confusingly like an exhaust backfiring; a split second later, the murderer had slammed the door shut and jumped clear. Had it not been for the lorry, Sponer would have turned around when he heard the bangs and seen the bastard jump clear. As it was, he hadn't turned around, and… But even if he had seen him, the man would still have jumped off and run away! But at least he could have claimed the man was wearing a brown coat, say, or he was tall perhaps, wearing a round hat; he could have seen him running off, he could have said the fellow looked such-and-such, but he just ran away. "What was I supposed to do? Run after him? He was going like a bat out of hell, Inspector! A man who jumps onto a moving car in the middle of the traffic and shoots someone!…" However, supposing he were to drive to a police station and simply say he'd seen the murderer jump off?… "Where, sir?"—"Right by the station, between the dark… between the patches of open ground…"—"What time?"— "Well, the train arrived at five minutes past the half hour, it's a couple of minutes to the exit, and then one, or at most two minutes on the road… It'd be about a quarter to…"— "Hell! A quarter to seven! It's already half past!"—"Half past seven?"—"Yes! Where have you been in the meantime?"— "Where have I been?…"—"And how did you get here from the Westbahnhof?"—"How did I get here?…"—"Yes! Didn't you stop immediately?"—"Yes, I did… no, yes… no, it wasn't at the West… it wasn't at the Westbahnhof at all, it happened in Währinger Strasse…"—"Did it now? Where did the man get in then?"—"Where?… Yes, he got in… he got in at the station, of course, but in the meantime I stopped…"—"Where did you stop in the meantime?"—"I broke down…"—"What was the matter?"—"I had a puncture…"—"And where in fact did the man ask you to take him? Hotel Bristol? How then did you manage to end up in the ninth district?"—"No, he wanted to go to… to Berggasse!"—"I see. What were you doing at the Opera House intersection in that case?"—"At the Opera?…"—"Yes, it says here in the report that you drove backwards and forwards like a madman over the Opera House intersection! You must have known at the time that the man was already dead, otherwise you wouldn't have panicked as you did…"—"Yes, I panicked…"—"For three-quarters of an hour? You heard shots, you saw a man jump off, you didn't stop, and only three-quarters of an hour—no, it's now nearly a whole hour—later, you come here and…"—"I really… I really panicked, I can't even think straight any longer, I don't even know… I…" He leant forward with a groan as though about to slump over the wheel to hide his face, but then threw himself back again, clenched his teeth, and banged a couple of times with his fist on the edge of the car door. He couldn't just carry on driving with the dead man in the car… He had to decide. He could no longer make a statement to the police. He had to get rid of the dead man.

Somewhere on the road, together with his luggage! Let the others, when they find him, work out for themselves how and when he'd been shot! He, Sponer, had nothing to do with it. Had he attacked him? No, it was rather the other way round. The chap had boarded an unsuspecting man's cab, had snuffed it there and left the driver to pick up the pieces. How? Very simply. Out you go, my fellow, in some dark spot, suitcases and all! You can't really expect me to do the decent thing, sit around for weeks, lose my job and get mixed up with the police, until, perhaps, one day they catch the real murderer. Or perhaps they won't. It's the least of my worries. You two can sort it out amongst yourselves!"

He looked around. He was now in the seventeenth district,

45

on the road to Dornbach. Fine! In the hills of Dornbach, between the villas, there were a number of lanes running through the gardens and the shrubbery, and poorly lit roads connecting the villas, where you hardly saw anyone after dark. He could stop there and, when the coast was clear, drag the dead man out, throw him onto the roadside, together with his bags, and clear off. He'd lie there till someone found him. They wouldn't know how he got there. They'd find out who he was, of course. He probably had some documents on him, a passport… But he, Sponer, could take care of that. They'd obviously open the suitcases and perhaps find something there, letters and such like, which would reveal the identity of the dead man… But one could throw the suitcases away somewhere else, a few hundred yards up the street… or perhaps right here, straight away? Maybe someone would see them lying there and simply take them home because of their contents. One doesn't look a gift horse in the mouth… But what if they are were handed in?

Why not take them to his lodgings instead?

Suppose, though, they did find out who the dead man was from his distinguishing features, for the police were trained in that sort of thing.

As far as he was concerned, what did it matter if they found out? But in fact it did… it did matter. Once they'd found out who the man was… "Arrived at the Westbahnhof. And? Took a taxi? Which one?" The other drivers, put on the spot, insist, "Not ours." But one of them could have seen Sponer drive up.

"Ferdinand Sponer from the Brandeis Garage."—"Did you pick up a fare?"—"Yes."—"What did he look like?"—"I don't know."—"You don't know?"—"No! He got in the cab when my back was turned, I only saw…"—"What did you see?"—"He was wearing an overcoat."—"What sort of overcoat?"—"A large grey one."—"And you saw nothing else?"—"No, all he said was…"—"What did he say?"—"He said… He said…"—"'The Bristol'," the porter intervenes.—"Yes, 'the Bristol'. Hotel Bristol."—"And what about you?"—"Me?… I took him there."—"To which one?"—"To… the old one."—"But when he got out and paid, you must have seen what he looked like."—"No… Yes. That is…"—"Well?"—"I don't remember precisely."—"OK, not precisely! But roughly. What do you remember roughly?"—"He… he wasn't very tall…"—"Not tall?"—"No."—"But not very short either?…"—"That's right."—"Roughly what age?"—"Not old."—"And what about his hair? Was it fair? Brown?"—"No, not fair… but not brown either…"—"Really? Not tall, not small, not old, not young, not fair, not brown? And what did he do when he got to the Bristol?"—"He paid the fare and went into the hotel."—"What about his suitcases?"—"A… a hotel porter took them from the cab."—"And went into the hotel with them, too?"—"Yes."—"What about you?"—"I drove off."—"So, he entered the hotel and the porter carried the suitcases in after him?"—"Yes."—"You saw all this?"—"Yes."—"Now, I put it to you that neither he nor his suitcases ever reached the hotel!"

If the body was found, he, Sponer, was lost.

Hundreds of people go missing in large cities every year. Without a trace. You don't hear about it, but they disappear. There's nothing in the newspapers about it. The papers report only the cases that have been solved. The unsolved ones are never reported in the papers. Hundreds of people, each one a grown person's height, size and weight, disappear like something small that falls to the ground, like a matchstick that one throws away, like a button that pops off and suddenly is no longer there. Gone. Vanished into thin air. As though it never existed.

How do they do it, how do they get rid of people? Do they cut them up, burn them somewhere, throw them into the river?

Into the river!

They say that a corpse thrown into the water first of all sinks, later rises to the surface for about half an hour, then sinks once more; but for a time it'll have been floating on the surface. If it's to stay under, it's got to be weighted down, and stones are best for this. In a fast-flowing river a body will be carried along by the flow; for a couple of days the corpse will float above the weights holding it down, it'll be swept along, fish will swim around it and nibble at it, it'll sink to the bottom, be buried and crushed in the debris, ground into pulp and be gone for ever.

Sponer had to throw the dead man into the Danube.

Not much more than an hour ago, he hadn't even known the man existed. Now that he no longer existed, he had to get rid of him somehow, because if the body were discovered it would be even more dangerous than if he'd murdered him, which, of course, he hadn't.

In order to turn back, he swung sharply to the left, but couldn't make a complete U-turn and had to reverse. A man in an overcoat, carrying an umbrella and a briefcase, very likely a lawyer who was here on business and wanted to get back to the centre, hailed him from the pavement. Sponer did not answer and sped away.

Seeing as it was raining, other people, too, had probably tried to hail him, but he hadn't noticed.

Now that he at least knew what he had to do, he began to think straight again. He could see where he was going. Previously he hadn't taken anything in.

The long rows of lamps swung to and fro over the wet, glistening streets. A strong wind had got up, and the rain was gradually beginning to ease off. The cloud cover was torn into white fluffy patches which raced over the pitch-black sky, now exposing, now concealing a full moon. Sponer could see this every time he crossed a wide intersection.

He glanced at his watch. It was a quarter past eight.

He slowed down. If he wanted to get to the Danube, he'd have to wait till he was sure he wouldn't meet anyone there.

When he approached the inner city, he turned right to make a detour and kill time, went through Josefstadt, and finally stopped in a side street off Burggasse, in the shadow of some dilapidated old houses.

There were only a few small shops, belonging to suburban shopkeepers, with heavy, old-fashioned doors. The pavements were narrow, the cobbled surface uneven. Some of the windows in the street were lit dimly from within, and every now and then the pale moonlight fell on the tall chimney stacks and grey walls of the houses, where here and there the stucco had come away in large patches.

The few passers-by paid no heed to Sponer and his car. A cat ran across the street, jumped over the steps of a doorway, and disappeared.

After a few minutes Sponer lit a cigarette.

Every time he drew on the cigarette the glow shone in the windscreen, the darkness behind Sponer's back being simultaneously reflected in front of him.

He threw the cigarette away and turned around.

The glass panels that separated him from the rear compartment were still slid back, with a gap of about two handbreadths between them.

Sponer forced himself to look into the back of the car.

In the slanting light of a distant street lamp he saw the rear seat, the edges of the suitcase and, between the two, like something incongruous, the blurred outlines of the slumped body.

The face was cadaverously pale. Because of the jolting during the journey, the head must have shifted even farther forward.

Just for a second he doubted that the man was still in the car. Every now and again he would be overcome by a sense of unreality. Sponer could well have imagined leaving the street, driving to a cab rank, picking up a fare, and opening the door for him. And in the car—nothing. The body and the luggage—a mere figment of the imagination.

But the suitcase next to the driver's seat was real enough.

He listened to see if anyone was coming, got out of the car, took the suitcase out, opened the rear door, and pushed the suitcase on top of the one that was already there. In the process, he avoided looking at the body. He quickly slammed the door and listened again.

As he was returning to his seat, it suddenly occurred to him that someone, a fare, could suddenly appear from behind while he was parked there, give an address, open the rear door and get in. Dammit! he thought.

He got back into his seat, pushed the glass panels even farther apart, and leant over into the interior.

He groped for the handles of the two doors and pushed them upwards so that the doors were locked and could no longer be opened from outside.

While he was leaning into the rear, he avoided breathing.

Then he pulled himself clear and sank back in his seat.


When he looked at his watch it was about nine.

He hadn't eaten anything since midday, but didn't feel at

all hungry; all he had was a hollow, uncomfortable sensation in his stomach.

If only he could find something to drink somewhere, he thought. He didn't want beer or wine, instead something like a sherry or vermouth.

He was already feeling a lot calmer, otherwise he wouldn't even have thought of such a thing. He'd have something later, say in about an hour's time, only now he had to drive to the Danube, throw the body and luggage into the river, and then he'd be safe.

While he sat there waiting, and while for a moment he had no need to think what to do next, he began to anticipate the sense of relief he'd feel after he'd got shot of his gruesome luggage, but at the same time he also felt he had to do something to relieve the tension of the last few hours.

If he could risk leaving the car unattended for a few minutes, he could go and get a drink somewhere.

After all, why shouldn't he leave the car unattended somewhere for a short time where it was dark? He'd been driving for almost two hours through the town, and no one had seen or even imagined the gruesome cargo he was ferrying. Besides, he'd left the car open by the Opera, at the crossing the policeman had shouted at him to move on, in Bräunerstrasse he'd left the car for nearly ten minutes right in front of the other policeman, and no one had even thought of suspecting him.

And let's face it, why should anyone suspect anything

dreadful to have happened right there in broad daylight rather than somewhere out in the outer suburbs, near some rubbish tip, under a bridge, places where traditionally such things are banished to and where, to be honest, you expect them to happen! Who, unless he'd experienced this sort of thing for himself, would imagine that it could occur right in front of one's eyes rather than behind the closed windows of a neighbour's house, behind the locked door of an adjoining room, among casual passers-by in the street, or anywhere at all for that matter! It is in the nature of horror to remain hidden and for no one to discover it. Anything outrageous is generally so private that everyone involved tries to hide the fact, and it is only fortuitously that it ever comes to light. Who can ever be aware of all the awful things that happen? Least of all the police.

He could be reported for careless driving across the Opera House junction, but that would be all, whereas to park here in this dark side street was perhaps the most reckless thing he'd done so far. Here, where without a doubt nothing happens from one year to the next, the police would patrol the neighbourhood most frequently. Surely no policeman would ever think of looking for crime in the open, in the glare of bright lights.

Sponer turned on the engine, drove out of the side street, and crossed Siebensterngasse and Mariahilfer Strasse.

The route he'd been driving with the dead man on board had now come full circle.

# 4

H E DROVE DOWN GETREIDEMARKT, past the fish market
and, just before he came to Wiedner Hauptstrasse,
stopped in a kind of a passageway between newly erected
trading stalls and shops.

He got out and tried both the rear door handles.

They were firmly locked.

Then, leaning across the steering-wheel, he pushed shut
the panels of the partition.

The car was all right here, in a sort of semi-darkness—not
where it was pitch black, which could arouse suspicion.

He glanced at the car once more, went over to the corner
of the street, turned, and found himself facing the brightly
lit shops of Wiedner Hauptstrasse.

Right there on the left was a slot-machine bar.

He went in.

It was a large, circular, dome-shaped room with slot
machines around the perimeter and tables in the middle at
which people were eating and drinking.

A radio was blaring.

He walked past the machines and studied the labels.

Over one of the taps was the inscription "Sherry".

He picked up a glass, held it under the tap, and inserted a coin in the slot.

The interior emitted a hollow gurgling and spluttering sound, and sherry—somewhat unappetisingly, he thought—gushed from the metal tap into the glass.

There are many people who don't enjoy the luxury of having dessert wines served up elegantly. Slot-machine bars are meant for the likes of them.

He picked up the glass, turned and leant his back against the railing of the machine. He took a gulp and looked around.

Next to him stood two girls seemingly perplexed in front of a fan-shaped, glass-covered carousel-type platter with sandwiches, so-called appetizers. Anything but, he thought. Did they want one?

Evidently. They were carrying on as if they didn't know what to do. They giggled and looked across as though expecting that Sponer would help them.

One of them was slim with sharp features and brown wavy hair, neatly arranged under a hat.

The memory of someone who had been adjusting her hair under her hat welled up in him—a lady in a dark suit with a fox fur slung over her shoulders, one foot delicately poised on the running board of his car, looking at herself in her mirror. He couldn't see her face, he only caught a glimpse of it in the mirror. Large grey eyes gazed at him from under a short veil.

When was that? Three days ago? He had a feeling it had been more like years.

He emptied the glass, put it down, mumbled something and stared at the floor.

The girls next to him laughed again.

"You couldn't show us," he suddenly heard one of them ask, "how you... how you work one of these machines... What you have to do?..." And the two laughed again, teasingly.

He raised his eyes. He hadn't yet looked at the one who had just spoken. She was above average height, very pretty, with a strikingly pale complexion, slightly spoilt by too much make-up, and platinum-blonde hair. Overall she gave the impression of being too spick and span, which irritated him as might the perfectly groomed hands of a manicurist in a salon.

Too much of a good thing, he thought. A pretty doll.

They both looked at him.

"You don't know what to do?" he asked.

"No," the blonde said, but very casually, as though she couldn't care less whether he believed her or not. He could see they weren't streetwalkers. Probably some office girls who were just enjoying themselves.

He leant over and took the coin that the blonde was holding.

The touch of her hand sent a shock up his arm.

The turmoil of the last few hours had made him react much more strongly to everything. The light, too, dazzled him, the music was deafening, the behaviour of the girls affected him more than he cared to admit, and the blonde, whom he'd probably have disregarded otherwise, suddenly embarrassed him.

He threw her a glance and let the money drop in the machine. The tray turned and dispensed a sandwich.

"Thank you," the blonde said, and took it from the machine.

The girls might have expected him to start up a conversation, but he said nothing. The blonde brought the sandwich to her mouth and took a bite. As she opened her lips, he saw her gleaming teeth.

"Are you going to stay?" the brunette asked at last.

"Here?"

"Yes. There'll be dancing now."

"Really?"

As they spoke, and while the radio continued to blare, a dance band consisting of four men stepped onto the stage. In the middle, between the tables, there was a free space, obviously the dance floor.

"Do you dance?" Sponer asked.

"Yes. And you?"

"Not very well," he said.

"We must have a go," she said. "Let's sit down at a table."

"I haven't got time," he mumbled.

"This won't take long."

He thought for a moment, then straightened up and said something like, "All right then."

The brunette smiled, and she and the blonde, who kept on eating as she listened, headed for one of the tables, followed by Sponer. They sat down, and the girls placed their handbags and gloves on the table. Then, while the brunette was taking off her coat and Sponer got up to help her, a waiter approached to take their orders.

The brunette, hanging her coat over the back of her chair, ordered a devilled egg.

The radio fell silent and the band struck up.

The blonde put the rest of her sandwich in her mouth, wiped her hands on her handkerchief and also took off her coat. The waiter asked for her order.

"What was that you were drinking?" she asked Sponer.

"Sherry," he said.

"I'll have one, too," she said to the waiter.

"And for you, sir?" the waiter asked.

"Same again," Sponer said, and sat down.

Some couples had already begun to dance.

"Aren't you going to take your coat off?" the brunette asked.

"No, the fact is," he mumbled, "I can't… I must be going soon." He pulled a packet of cigarettes from his pocket and offered one to the girls. The brunette declined, but the blonde helped herself, and while he was giving her a light, a young man, obviously a clerk or the like, approached her and asked her for a dance. She put the cigarette down and got up.

Sponer lit his, and the blonde and her partner walked onto the dance floor and began to dance.

"Pity you don't want to dance," the brunette said.

"Well," Sponer said, but just then the waiter appeared with their orders. The girl asked for some bread, which was passed to her, and she began to eat. Sponer looked across to the blonde. He concluded she was the prettiest one there. He took a sip from the glass. The music stopped, but started up again after the dancers had clapped a few times.

While he kept looking at the dancers, Sponer suddenly again had a feeling of total unreality, this time not about what had happened, but what was actually happening. It struck him as totally incredible that, after driving like a madman for two hours with the dead man through the whole town, he should now be sitting with the girls, drinking and smoking; or, to be more precise, with his spirits raised by the music and the alcohol, he could momentarily no longer dissociate the deed of the stranger and his own flight from the consequences that were bound to follow. Since he hadn't observed the actual murder and indeed hadn't even seen the murderer, he was pretty sure that as soon as the crime was discovered it'd be put at his door, so that in the end he began to feel as though he had in fact perpetrated it himself. And had he really been the murderer, in all probability he wouldn't have been behaving any differently from the way he was now. He'd just be sitting with the two girls, smoking and drinking. One knows how often criminals, after committing a crime, seek the company of women simply in order to forget.

The brunette may well have tried to engage him in small talk a couple of times, and he might have replied without thinking, but just then she repeated something to which he had apparently not responded. "There's something on your sleeve," he heard her repeat.

He glanced down. She had got hold of the right-hand sleeve of his coat and was looking at the material. There were a couple of dark stains at the bottom edge.

It was dried blood.

He shuddered. "Get out of here!" a voice cried within him. "Now! Immediately!"

"Oh," he said with apparent unconcern, though haltingly, "it's… it's nothing. Just some… p-paint. Th-that's all it is." He pretended to look at it and at the same time felt sweat break out on his forehead. He stood up. "I-I'll…" he stuttered, "I must… wash it off with some water…"

"Come with me," she said, "I'll do it for you." And she, too, was about to get up. "There's bound to be some warm water in the kitchen…"

"No," he said. "Thanks all the same. Don't worry. I'll… I'll be back in just a second…"

"But it's no trouble," she interjected.

"Just don't worry!" he said. He had already taken a few

steps from the table, but came back and without a word picked up his cap, which he had left behind.

The girl looked at him in amazement.

He ignored her, reached into his pocket, tossed a couple of coins on a table as he passed, and made for the exit. He almost ran the last few steps. He indicated to a waiter, who had suddenly appeared in front of him, where he had thrown the money. As he did so he could see the brunette still staring at him goggle-eyed. Next moment he was out on the street.

Rain glistened in the light of the street lamps.

He ran to the right and turned the corner.

A man was standing by his cab, and had his hand next to the steering wheel as he kept honking the horn for all he was worth.

"Cabby!" he shouted as Sponer rounded the corner.

Sponer was at his side in a flash.

"What the hell do you think you're doing!" he hissed, and yanked the man's hand away from the horn.

"You weren't here!" the man yelled back. "You think I like standing out in the rain? Metternichgasse, number nine!" and he reached for the door handle as if to get in.

Sponer jumped in and turned on the engine.

"The door won't open!" the man shouted. Instead of answering, Sponer engaged second gear, put his foot down and sped off.

The man tumbled back and swore after him.

\*

Driving at speed along Wiedner Hauptstrasse, Sponer lifted up his arm to have a look at the stains on the sleeve.

"Dammit!" he swore.

At Paulanerkirche he turned left.

Not to have noticed the blood! Perhaps there were more stains on his suit and collar. He turned the mirror and looked. As the street lights flashed past, he saw only his white face with its dilated eyes, almost dark blue, lighting up and dimming at intervals.

He didn't even notice that he had crossed Alleegasse. At the Schwarzenberg Palace he slowed down.

The large clock over the ring road showed nearly ten.

He drove down Lastenstrasse.

The interior of the car was full of blood, too, no doubt—the seat, the carpet! And the bullets, after passing through the body, must be lodged somewhere in the upholstery!

This man had messed up everything with his death.

The blood could be washed off, though one would have to explain away the damage. How though? Surely he'd find a way, provided the dead man and his luggage were disposed of, provided they simply weren't there any more. As if they'd never existed, neither the man nor his cases. "A Mr So-and-so?"—"No record of him here."—"He travelled to Vienna?"—"Definitely not."—"And he didn't check in?"—"He didn't check in anywhere."—"Did he check out at the other end?"—"Yes, but didn't arrive here."—"When did he leave?"—"Tuesday."—"Really? Time of

arrival?"—"Eighteen thirty-five… at the Westbahnhof."—
"Yes, he should have been on that train, but the fact is he
wasn't…"—"What?"—"The drivers?"—"Yes, one of them…
Yes, the porter said that… Yes, to the Bristol."—"But that
must've been someone else. Nobody by that name had
checked in at the hotel…"—"What do you mean, nobody
had checked in?…"—"He must've though, but…"—"What
was the driver's name?"—"Ferdinand Sponer."—"I beg your
pardon?"—"Yes, of course."—"Yes, sir, certainly. We'll bring
him in for questioning."

There could be mail waiting at the Bristol, which was no
longer being picked up; there could have been meetings
arranged, which someone had failed to attend; someone
might have been expected, but hadn't turned up. In each
and every case they would notice a person was missing,
and in each case they'd finally ask Sponer, "Where is he?"

He who had imagined he was lost if the body were found
now realized he was lost if the dead man didn't turn up safe
and well at the hotel.

Having sized up the situation, he stopped agonizing. He
simply went into action.

He drove up Lastenstrasse, turned into Marxergasse,
crossed the Rotunden Bridge over the Danube Canal and,
taking Rustenschacherallee, ended up in Lusthausstrasse.

The huge oaks and poplars in the Prater rustled in the
wind and rain.

Just before the second flower-bed island in the road, he

63

emerged onto Hauptallee. At the Lusthaus—the Pavilion—he had planned to drive up Enzersdorfer Allee, a potholed street, overgrown with grass and lined with ancient trees, but changed his mind when he spotted a mounted policeman on patrol, who could have stopped to ask him what he was up to on that bumpy, almost impassable pitch-black road.

Consequently, he took the right fork along the Poloplatz and the stands of the Freudenauer racecourse till he reached the Danube Canal again and finally ended up at some warehouses where he was able to turn left once more and go back the way he had come, thereby making a circuit of the racecourse. The roads here were no more than raised gravel embankments, poorly lit as was to be expected in the middle of the meadow lands. A disused tramline ran in the centre of the road.

He drove along the railings of the racecourse, under a cluster of trees which rustled in the wind, turned off into a short, dark track that abruptly became bumpy, and finally came to a wide hollow about six foot deep, densely overgrown with leafless shrubs. Instead of leaves, the shrubs were thickly covered with clumps and bunches of wine-red autumn berries. Caught in the beams of his headlights, a veritable sea of bright red and crimson suddenly lit up in the pouring rain. He resolutely drove over to where the shrubbery was less dense. Creepers became entangled in the wheels of his car.

He turned off all the lights, pushed the interior partitions

64

apart and reached again into the interior to release one of the door handles. Then he got out and opened the door.

Darkness, redolent of death, enshrouded him. The rain drummed on the roof of the car and soaked his cap and overcoat.

He leant inside and struck a match. The corpse, shaken into an untidy heap, lay between the seat and the suitcases.

Sponer transferred the match to his left hand, and with his right hand took hold of the man's hair and pulled him up by his head till his body sagged over backwards.

He now saw that the man was about his own age, clean-shaven, with features which, but for the wan pallor and the bloodstains, would not have been unattractive. A pair of greenish, half-shut eyes stared vacantly back at him.

He dropped the match which had burned to the end, struck another, and began to empty the man's pockets as quickly as he could. In the breast pockets he found a passport and a couple of letters; in the waistcoat—a bundle of keys; in the overcoat pockets—cigarettes, a lighter and two French newspapers; in the left trouser pocket—some silver coins and a couple of loose, short cartridges; in the right—a handkerchief; in the left hip pocket—a wallet; and in the right hip pocket—a short-barrelled large-calibre revolver.

The man had clearly tried to reach for it, because Sponer had seen the dead man sitting with both hands on his right hip before the body collapsed in a heap. Sponer took all these things. They were partly blood-stained, as the whole of the dead man's waistcoat was soaked in blood that had already turned sticky.

Apart from the bullet holes in his throat, the man had two more in his upper chest.

In the corner, where he had been sitting, three holes could also be seen: one in the roof lining which stretched right down to the top of the armrest, and two in the upholstery of the armrest.

Sponer got out, went in the dark to the rear and felt the bodywork to see if he could find the exit holes. He only found one, through the roof. The other two bullets had obviously not penetrated the car body. They might have become lodged somewhere. They were probably lead, rather than steel ones.

Sponer struck another match to try and throw some light on the shrubbery in the hollow. There were a lot of loose stones and gravel that had rolled down from the road.

After the match had gone out, he began to scoop up the stones with his bare hands, take them to the car and stuff them in the dead man's pockets. Every now and again he'd listen, but there was no sound apart from the wind and rain.

He filled the dead man's pockets as far as he could with the stones, including those of the overcoat. Finally, he also stuffed stones down the trouser legs, which he then tied fast at the bottom with his own coat belt to prevent the stones falling out, and looped the ends of the belt round both legs.

He wiped his hands on the man's overcoat, stood for a couple of moments in the darkness, slammed the rear door shut, got back into the driver's seat, switched on the lights and turned on the engine again.

It took him a few attempts to mount the embankment which, in the headlights, rose sharply in front of him. The wheels kept sinking deeper and deeper into the soft ground, but finally, after he had backed a little and had got some speed up, the car cleared the slope and came onto the road again.

For a distance he drove towards the city centre, then turned left at an abandoned, dilapidated inn on the quay, the Winterhafen, and passed a kind of wooden outhouse, no longer in use, like the rest of the buildings on the Winterhafen. There were only two old barges there, but without their crew, who were probably sleeping somewhere in the city rather than on board.

Another hundred yards and he found himself on the Danube.

He pulled up next to the railway line.

The river, glistening under the night sky, surged past with a soft, menacing power.

Sponer turned off the engine and lights, and listened. All that was to be heard was the patter of the rain and the surge of the river.

The lights of some houses shone a long distance away.

Sponer slowly got out of his cab. After standing still for a few seconds, he suddenly swung open the rear door, reached into the darkness and dragged the corpse out. The body, weighed down with the stones, was inordinately heavy.

Sponer couldn't carry it. Holding it under the arms, he dragged it as fast as he could to the edge of the road, over the railway line and down the stony embankment. There he paused for a moment, breathing heavily. Then he pushed the body into the water.

But it remained where it was at the river's edge. It was too heavy for him to lift up and throw into deeper water.

He therefore had to resolve to wade into the water himself and drag the body after him. He threw off his overcoat and took a few steps into the river. The bank dropped steeply, and the water almost immediately came up to his chest. It was ice-cold, and he nearly lost his footing in the current.

He grabbed hold of the dead man again and pulled the corpse towards him. He could feel the current tugging at the body. He took one more step into the deep water and then let go. With a slight gurgle the body disappeared. He himself was almost swept away. He threw himself towards the bank, felt himself being picked up by the current, but managed to hold onto some stonework, drew himself onto the embankment and, a bit farther downstream, emerged out of the water. He was soaked to the skin. He looked for his overcoat, found it, put it on, and clambered up the embankment.

He cast a quick look around. Nothing. Then he glanced again down the river. The rippling, swirling torrent rushed past at speed.

The dead man was gone.

The rain would wash away the trail of blood leading from the car to the water's edge…

Sponer washed the blood from the interior of the car at one of the few Danube tributaries that could still be seen here and there in the marshy meadows, collecting into small ponds or pools.

Then he lifted the two suitcases onto the seat, felt for the gloves which he had thrown into the rear at the Opera House, found them and stuck them in his coat pocket. He removed the fibre mat and inspected it by the light of a match.

There were a few dark spots, but not many. The dead man's clothing must have soaked up most of the blood.

Suddenly Sponer caught sight of the man's hat lying before him on the running board. It had very likely rolled out when he was pulling out the floor mat.

Sponer took the mat to the edge of the pond, threw it in the water and pushed it under. Then he picked up the hat, placed a stone inside, tore off the band, tied it up so that the stone couldn't fall out, and threw the lot into the pond. The bundle struck the water with a splash and sank.

Sponer looked for a rag in one of the side pockets next to the driver's seat, dipped it in water, and began to wash the blood from the leather upholstery. He wrung the rag out, dipped it again in water, and washed the upholstery once more, in addition to the floor and the suitcases. He repeated this several times.

After that, he threw the rag into the reeds, pulled out the mat from the water, rinsed it, wrung it out, and replaced it in the car. He positioned the suitcases on the floor, struck another match, and looked into the back. There was no more blood to be seen.

He looked at the bullet holes once more by the light of a match, pulled out his penknife and picked at the edge of the holes until they lost their characteristic appearance and it looked as if the upholstery and roof had been damaged in some other way.

He listened all the while in case anyone was coming. But there was no one. Once, two cars sped past above on the road. That was all.

That the inside of the car was wet, he could explain by the rainy weather and the wet shoes and clothes of his fares.

And where the upholstery was damaged, he'd say it had just split. After all, the cab was not new; it had been formerly converted from a private car.

By the time he left the Prater, it was almost eleven. He now had to hurry.

First he drove to his flat, stopping at the corner of the street rather than right up at the house.

He took the suitcases out of the car, carried them to the

front door, opened it and, with the suitcases in his hands, groped his way up the dark stairs.

He stopped in front of his flat and listened. It was dark on the other side of the glass door panels; his landlord, as was to be expected, was already fast asleep.

He unlocked the door, quickly crossed the entrance hall and walked into his room. He put the suitcases down and switched on the light. Then he went back and closed both doors.

He took off his overcoat. His suit was soaking wet, and so was the inside of the overcoat.

He took the dead man's belongings out of his pockets and put them on the table. They, too, were wet to some extent, and only the passport, wallet and the letters, which he had placed in his breast pocket, had stayed almost dry.

He opened the passport.

It was American, issued in Chicago, in the name of one Jack Mortimer, bachelor, citizen of the United States, born on 12th November 1899, occupation not specified, oval face, grey eyes, brown hair.

On page three was a stamped photograph of the dead man, jejune like all passport photos; a fairly young man with slicked-back hair, signed underneath: Jack Mortimer.

Jack Mortimer!

Without taking his eyes off the passport, Sponer began to undress. He opened the wallet. Inside was some Austrian money—not a lot, a couple of hundred-franc notes and a book of traveller's cheques.

He took the letters. There were three, written in English and fairly short.

Naked, he held them to the light and tried to read them. They had no heading and were signed only with a W.

The addressee was Jack Mortimer, Hotel Royal, Paris. They bore French stamps and had been franked in Paris.

They were love letters.

He began to feel cold; he took the bunch of keys and opened both suitcases. Underwear, clothing and personal belongings, thrown together haphazardly, tumbled forth.

He decided that he'd go through it all later; for the time being he just took a dark-grey suit, a pair of black shoes and some underwear.

The shirt that he put on was too tight at the neck, so he took one of his own out of the wardrobe and put it on. The shoes were slightly too large, but they would do. The jacket was a shade too narrow around the shoulders and the sleeves were about an inch too long. But he could wear them, all the same.

He chose a dark-red tie belonging to the dead man and put it on.

Then he took his own wet clothes except for the overcoat and locked them in the wardrobe. He removed the key. He washed the overcoat sleeve in the washbasin to remove the bloodstains—likewise the gloves, which he withdrew from the pocket—put the overcoat on even though it was still damp, put his cap on, and stuffed the man's things as well as his own into his pockets. Then he turned off the light, left the room, locked it from the outside and put the key in his pocket.

He felt his way down the dark stairs, left the house and returned to his car.

He got in and drove three houses farther on to his garage, a large, roofed, dimly lit yard, at the entrance to which someone was still washing a car.

He asked the man why he was still at it so late.

The man mumbled that the car had to be ready first thing in the morning.

Sponer nodded in reply.

He looked at his watch. It was almost midnight. Just then Georg Haintl walked into the garage to take over from him.

He had probably been in a bar, because he smelt of wine.

Sponer let him have the car together with the day's takings. He paid with his own money what Jack Mortimer hadn't. Or was it Jack Mortimer's money he paid with? He didn't know, the silver had got mixed up in his pocket.

"What's that tie you've got on?" Haintl asked.

"Oh," said Sponer, "it's a new one. By the way," he added, "the upholstery's damaged."

"Yes?" enquired Haintl.

"That's right," said Sponer. He opened the door and showed Haintl the damage. Haintl leant into interior, examined the upholstery and mumbled something.

"The car's getting old," said Sponer. "Show it to Brandeis in the morning."

Brandeis was the proprietor's son. He, too, sometimes drove the cars. Brandeis was to take over from Haintl at seven in the morning, and then Sponer would take over at midday.

Haintl, without commenting on the fact that the interior of the car was wet, drew his head back, and Sponer shut the door.

They stood there for a moment, looking at the car. For one that had been driven in the city, it was excessively spattered with mud.

However, before Haintl could comment on this, Sponer quickly said goodbye and left.

He hurried back to his house, opened the front door, went up the stairs and entered his room once more.

He flung his coat and cap on the bed, but then stuck the cap in his overcoat pocket. He began yet again to rummage through Mortimer's suitcases; he pulled out a light overcoat and a hat which happened to be rather crumpled, but he straightened it out and put it on. It came down over his ears a bit. He tore a strip off one of the two French newspapers which were still lying there and stuffed it under the lining. Now the hat fitted him. He put on Mortimer's coat, locked the suitcases, slung his driver's coat over his arm, picked up the cases and left the room.

He left the room door unlocked, but locked the door to the flat; he then carried the suitcases down the stairs and stepped out onto the street.

He had to carry the suitcases for about ten minutes till he saw an empty taxi, which he hailed.

"Südbahnhof," he said, taking a good look at the driver.

The journey took about twelve minutes. At the station he got out, paid, waived a porter, and entered the station with the cases in his hands. In one of the halls he put down the cases by a side exit, threw his coat on top and waited a couple of minutes. In the meantime he smoked a cigarette. Then he picked up his things again and left the station by the exit leading into the city.

Here he took a cab.

"New Bristol," he said.

A few minutes later the car stopped by the Bristol at the same spot where earlier he himself ought to have pulled up with Jack Mortimer.

The hotel entrance was still lit; to the right shone the red and light-blue neon sign of the hotel bar.

While Sponer was paying, a hotel attendant approached.

Sponer nodded, and the man, having greeted him, lifted the cases out of the car and carried them to the entrance.

Sponer glanced at the driver. With the coat over his arm he then entered the hotel.

The glittering marble hall dazzled him for a second. The thick pile of the carpets absorbed all sound of footsteps. Strains of dance music reached him from somewhere intermittently.

A liveried porter came up to him.

Sponer said, "My name's Jack Mortimer."

The porter bowed immediately. "We had been expecting you about seven, sir." And straight away he added something else in English, which Sponer failed to understand.

"I was held up," Sponer muttered.

Another man, in a suit, suddenly stood before him.

"Mr Mortimer?" he asked. "This way please!" And he noiselessly hurried towards a lift door. Sponer followed. They entered the lift. A bellboy was suddenly at his side to take the overcoat from his arm. The lift started, then stopped. They got out. They walked along carpeted, glittering marble corridors. A door was swung open, a chandelier lit up, mirrors of a salon gleamed all round, a bedroom with brocade bed covers was illuminated, snow-white walls, nickel and chrome fittings shone in a bathroom, and the soft-spoken manager—addressing him now in English, now in German, eager to explain and recommend—bowed again, taking a step backwards to allow a second small boy to hand Sponer his mail, comprising a few letters and two telegrams.

"Would Sir require anything else," Sponer heard the manager ask.

Sponer shook his head. If there was anything else he wanted he'd ring, he muttered; and the manager, the man who brought the luggage, and the two boys bowed and disappeared.

He was left standing in the middle of the room, in Mortimer's room, in Mortimer's clothes, in Mortimer's life.

And in his hand he held Mortimer's letters. He planned to spend a night in the dead man's life and be gone the next morning, no matter where, disappear, become himself again, Sponer, the taxi driver who had delivered Mortimer alive and well at the Bristol, and whom no one could accuse if he was later asked, "Where is he? Where's Jack Mortimer?" Hadn't he arrived at the Bristol with his luggage, spent a night, and left the following day?—Where to?—None of my business! How should I know? Go and ask someone else! He left my cab and went into the hotel; how should I know what he did after that?

For one night only he would live Mortimer's life, and the next morning he'd return to his own. Because otherwise people might turn up who knew Mortimer, or who had business to discuss that only Mortimer could handle, or a question to put to him to which only Mortimer knew the answer.

But he, Sponer, wouldn't be there any more. The dead man's life into which he had stepped would be over in a few hours.

But that's not how things turned out. It was no longer a question of hours. One doesn't step into anyone's life, not even a dead man's, without having to live it to the end.

He, Sponer, was now Jack Mortimer, the living. And that's how he would have to stay, right up to Mortimer's death.

# 5

H E KEPT STARING at the floor, and only after the
people had left, did he dare raise his eyes, fixing
them on the closed door and listening for every sound.
He waited until the door to the corridor had fallen shut,
for only then did he imagine he'd be safe till morning.
Then, suddenly, he heard a noise which told him they
were still on the other side of the door; he even heard the
manager issuing an instruction and one of the bellboys
answering him. The manager said something further, and
this time it was the porter who answered; then a couple
of voices spoke simultaneously. All of a sudden, however,
they stopped as if by command, or rather, continued in
a whisper; he heard it clearly even though he couldn't
understand what they were saying. But the whispering
continued.

While he was listening, his heart went on beating faster
and faster, and in the end he couldn't stand it any more. He
rushed noiselessly to the door and pressed his ear against it,
but he still couldn't understand anything. Finally his nerves
snapped and he threw the door open.

He saw the manager, the bellboys and the porter standing

in the hallway, looking at a picture in a gilt frame, which took up a large part of the wall.

It was an old oil painting depicting a battle scene.

A suite of furniture—a silk-covered sofa and two armchairs, which had stood under the painting—had been pushed aside.

As Sponer flung the door open, he saw them stare back in terror. The manager immediately began to apologize. "It wasn't hanging straight," he said, motioning towards the picture. At the same time, at a nod from him, the suite was pushed back where it belonged, and they quickly left the room, bowing.

After the door had closed, Sponer wiped his brow with his sleeve. Then he suddenly threw the letters that he was still holding in his hand onto the sofa, ran to the door, opened it, tore the key out of the lock, double locked the door from inside, turned round, and was about to take a deep breath and say to himself, "Now I'm safe till the morning..."

Instead, from the moment he locked the door, he had the overwhelming feeling that he was in a trap and that everywhere people were lying in wait and eavesdropping on him.

His nerves, which had held firm for six hours, and which had endured the car journey through the city with the dead man on board, the sinking of the body, and the desperate risk of adopting Mortimer's identity, finally snapped the moment when there was nothing else to do but wait for the next morning.

First of all, however, he tried to suppress his anxiety. He walked slowly up to the painting, looked at it and fingered the frame, causing it to sway slightly. He lifted it away from the wall and let it fall back with a slight clatter. He even knelt on the sofa to examine it in more detail.

A large body of cavalry and foot soldiers clad in clothes of antiquity were marching through dark clouds of smoke. The baroque motif of a white charger with a swanlike neck and a huge crupper pointing towards the foreground caught his attention in particular. Staring fixedly—to block out all other thoughts—at the shooting, stabbing and the general mêlée portrayed in the painting, he pulled off his overcoat and threw it aside. He was feeling unbearably hot. He gulped two or three times, as if to swallow something that had become lodged in his throat. The black, piercing, mouselike eyes of the rider, looking over his shoulder, on the pirouetting white charger, stared out at him penetratingly from the small, weather-beaten face; also, when he got up from the sofa and stepped back, they appeared to follow him everywhere, and he had the feeling he was suffocating in this over-richly decorated, but relatively small room. Everything was eerily silent; the plush carpets absorbed every sound. He drew his hand once again over his forehead, went back to the salon, but then, after a quick look round, returned immediately to the bedroom, from there went to the bathroom, and found himself once again in the hallway. However, he didn't stay there but walked, or rather ran, again into the salon and bedroom, into the bathroom and hallway, and repeated this mad circuit three or four times, each time faster and faster; the furniture and lights swam in front of his eyes, forming a swirling pattern, until he tripped over the edge of a rug and fell with a crash.

He remained lying there utterly still for a few moments, then turned over with a groan, let his head drop back, and stared wide-eyed about the room as if unaware of what had happened.

Lying on his back, it seemed as if something had snapped inside him, for he suddenly felt easier and also felt the coolness of the floor doing him good. He now perceived everything with unusual clarity, probably on account of his posture, each object making a greater and more powerful impression upon him than before.

The room was sumptuously decorated, mainly in the First Empire style, though in other styles as well, and all around him he could see highly polished furniture, caryatides adorned with lights, and wallpaper reaching up to the ceiling. A greenish bronze chandelier with three tiers of light bulbs swayed overhead, and the wooden ceiling was divided into uniform diamond-shaped figures, each displaying a fantastic, lavishly painted, gilt and silvered coat of arms. Leopards, eagles and lilies intertwined to form an overbearing ornamentation that would have been more appropriate as a feature in a funeral parlour.

Still shaking slightly, he stood up and walked over to the

bedroom as if to recommence his tour, interrupted by the fall, but halted at the door. The room was done out in wine-red velvet, and over the bed hung a gold-coloured silk baldachin. On the bedcover a gold-embroidered pomegranate pattern shimmered in the dim light of two pendant lamps which, like at a catafalque, shone either side of the bed—Mortimer's bed. He could easily imagine the outstretched form of the murdered man in the shadow of the baldachin.

The anxiety, which to some extent had abated with the fall, now surged back; it rose, as it were, from the floor up to his knees, gobbling up his whole body, and began, in a probing and insidious manner, to go for his throat, choking him. Mortimer's life confronted him in a more ghostly, weird and threatening manner than Mortimer's death.

Till now he hadn't had a single spare moment to think about who this Mortimer in fact was; these rooms, which Mortimer had never entered, seemed to know, and were trying to impart to him who Mortimer was. In vain did he keep reminding himself that this no longer concerned him, that come the morning he would be out of the hotel, that he would forget Mortimer like a bad dream. But the air was saturated with the presence of the dead man who had no wish to stay dead; it was as if he were already here, lying in wait for Sponer. Now that he had latched onto him, he didn't want to lose this last chance to carry on living; he was assailing Sponer, clinging onto him, sapping his lifeblood; he was not to be shaken off.

A dead man is simply that; he decays and disappears; soon it is as if he had never existed. The dead man who had lain in his car was being swept along by the river, attacked by fish, ground to pulp by rocks and boulders; he was floating downstream towards Hungary; soon he would be less than a stain in the water or a rustle in the reeds. He was gone, had vanished, the corpse was by now miles away—so far so good. However, it was ridiculous to suppose that as a result anything had been accomplished. The real Mortimer was not dead at all. He continued to live.

He was very much alive, and there was no need for him to look anything like the former Mortimer—a young man of about thirty, medium height, bland features, hair slicked back, eyes grey. He might as well look like Sponer now, though it was immaterial what he looked like; all he yearned for was to live, irrespective of whether he looked like this or like that, had fair hair or brown hair, grey or dark-blue eyes. It was no longer a question of hair or eyes, face, hands or body, he had settled in Sponer's skull. Like a bird of prey he had sunk his claws into this, his new nest, and had implanted himself there; he could no longer be shooed away; he ruled and gave the orders: lift up your hand, do this, do that, bestir yourself, stop, take me there, follow my commands, do as I wish! For are you not me now?

For a man is not just a thing of flesh and blood that walks, eats, drinks, sleeps and dies; rather a man is that what is in the minds of others, whom he loves or hates, commands, insults, seduces, confuses, destroys, preoccupies and torments. Mortimer was no longer the dead man in the river, he was the demon in Sponer's head. It had taken only a few hours to shove Mortimer's corpse out of the way; the living Mortimer was a far trickier customer to deal with.

Sponer, who somehow had to survive, was now floundering in the dark, beset from all quarters by dangers as if by wild beasts, ready to attack him at any moment. He simply no longer believed that when he left the hotel in the morning, it would be the end of the matter. There was more to come. There always was.

It would persist—he could no longer get away from it—yet he didn't have the faintest idea what it was. He was hooked. Perhaps the suitcases contained something that would give him a clue? He tore them open, pulled out the articles one by one, and scattered them over the chairs. Underwear, suits, toiletries, shoes; some items were still quite new or hardly used. It seemed as if the dead man had recently kitted himself out, everything seemed quite impersonal, just like any other man's wardrobe, as if the dead man didn't want to betray himself. Sponer searched through all the pockets, looking for letters, but found nothing, and then he remembered the mail they'd given him when he arrived at the hotel, and he had already forgotten what he'd done with it, but finally he found it in the entrance hall on the sofa where he'd thrown it. He first tore open the telegrams, read two incomprehensible and obviously coded messages in English, chucked them aside, opened one of the letters and, while searching with his free hand in his jacket pocket for cigarettes, lowered himself onto the edge of the sofa and began to study the letter, all the while continuing to fumble unsuccessfully for his cigarettes. However, he didn't understand the letter as he didn't know much English. He tore open the second, which, like the two in Mortimer's wallet, was again signed with a W, and deduced it was another love letter. He returned to the salon, looked to see whether perhaps he'd thrown the cigarette packet away somewhere, and in the meantime removed the dead man's wallet and compared the handwriting of the old letters with the new one; it was the same. However, he didn't continue reading, because not being able to find his cigarettes infuriated him suddenly. He hadn't been in need of a smoke at all so far; now, however, he was all of a sudden dying for one and, unable to find his cigarettes, he blew his top. Swearing furiously, he rushed to the door and rang for the waiter.

Scarcely had he done this than the danger of the situation dawned upon him. The waiter might of course know him, for he might already have met the man, God knows where, but it was a distinct possibility, or alternatively the waiter might know Mortimer. That the staff in the entrance hall didn't was beside the point, for the staff might have changed, or there might be another shift on duty, especially at night. So, if a room bell was rung, the waiter was not to know, even if he had met Mortimer previously, that the person now in the

85

room should be Mortimer; the bell had simply rung for room number such-and-such, and when the waiter entered and encountered someone other than Mortimer, why should he suspect that he, Sponer, was impersonating anyone! In the morning, however, at checkout, staff who knew Mortimer might well be on duty. He, Sponer, would of course just hurry past them and get in the car, but all the same, someone could notice that the person getting in was not the Mortimer he knew. The car would of course immediately drive off, but the busybody trying to match Sponer's appearance with that of Mortimer's would be puzzled, questions might be asked, and if it later turned out that Mortimer had disappeared, everyone would say, "Yes, we, too, found he looked quite different," and they'd follow this lead and enquire what time he had arrived, why only after midnight if the train was in before seven p.m., and then they'd enquire further and ask who had driven him from the Westbahnhof, and the drivers would come up for questioning again. Damn! However, so much time would have elapsed, days and weeks probably, before they'd discover Mortimer's disappearance that they'd no longer be able to establish who had been at the station that time… What, however, if they found out sooner that he had disappeared? Perhaps people were already expecting him, he might have acquaintances in the city, perhaps he'd actually been here before, of course, otherwise the porter wouldn't have…

His thoughts, which were again in a welter of confusion, were interrupted by a knock at the door. Who was it? The waiter? Why didn't he just enter? Sponer stood there in silence. The knocking was repeated.

"What's the matter?" he finally shouted out.

Somebody was saying something on the outside, and at the same time the door handle moved up and down. He'd forgotten that he had locked the door and, despite his utterly confused state, he suddenly realized he was behaving like a madman; the dead man's belongings were lying all over the chairs and strewn around on the floor. He picked some of them up quickly and stuffed them into the suitcases.

"Just a moment!" he called to the person on the other side of the door, smoothed his hair, looked in the mirror to straighten his tie, and was horrified by what he saw. A face stared back at him, for all the world like the dead man's. Closing his eyes for a second, he smoothed his hair down once more, went to the door, unlocked and opened it, ready to slam it shut immediately if it turned out that he knew the person standing there.

The waiter who entered was, however, a complete stranger. He was a man of about thirty-eight or forty, clean-shaven, unruffled in appearance, and on the portly side. He asked how he could be of help.

"Cigarettes!" Sponer said.

"Khedive, Figaro, Dimitrino, Simon Arzt?" the waiter asked, and looked at Sponer.

Under the waiter's gaze Sponer began once more to straighten his tie, and again brushed back his hair from his forehead, but when he looked up and saw the waiter still staring, he felt the blood rush to his head.

He was gripped by sudden fury.

"What are you looking at?" he asked the man.

"I beg your pardon?" the waiter enquired.

"What are you looking at?" Sponer shouted.

"Looking at?" the waiter stuttered.

"Yes, looking at!" Sponer shouted.

"Nothing," the startled waiter stammered. "I'm not… looking at anything."

"Well then!"

Sponer swung round and, infuriated, took a couple of steps towards the salon, tugged again at his tie, turned round, approached the waiter and looked at him intently. The man was now gazing at the floor.

"So what was it you said?" Sponer finally asked.

The waiter repeated the brands of the cigarettes.

"Khedive," Sponer ordered. The others were unfamiliar to him.

The waiter bowed immediately and left.

Sponer watched him leave, swore under his breath, and returned to the salon.

When he entered, he saw the cigarette packet he had been looking for, lying on the table.

It was Mortimer's.

He had no idea how it had got there. It might have dropped out of his pocket when he fell.

He pulled a cigarette from the packet and lit it.

It was honey-flavoured.

He took a couple of puffs and then went up to the mirror again. He was still as pale as a sheet. His pupils were fully dilated and his eyes shone with a black-blue lustre in the glass of the mirror, and everything else that was reflected behind him—the room and the lights—glittered and swam in a kind of vitreous haze. The cigarette smoke stung his eyes, he closed them and took another puff; at the same time, a tingling sensation in his hands began to travel up his arms, and when he opened his eyes again the reflection in the mirror had gone out of shape. Overcome by dizziness, he turned; there was a rushing sound in his ears, the roots of his hair felt as though they were frozen in ice, and the lights in the room faded. A ringing, like a multitude of bells took over, and bright flesh-coloured pinkish objects swam in and out of his field of vision, constantly changing shape; he suddenly felt the carpet rise to meet his hands and knees; he was not aware of collapsing, he just felt that someone had caught him under his arms, was dragging him across the floor and propping up in an armchair.

It was the waiter, returning with the cigarettes, who had seen him collapse.

Then followed an interval which he no longer remembered; finally he noted the waiter was saying something repeatedly; yet he understood nothing. At last it dawned on him that the man was asking whether he should fetch a glass of brandy.

Meanwhile something like an enormous cloud lifted from his consciousness.

"No, thank you, not brandy," he murmured in answer to the repeated question.

It must have been the cigarette that had caused him to faint, he babbled. He hadn't eaten anything for a long time... on the journey, he added.

The waiter asked whether he should bring him something from the bar, maybe a cutlet or fillet steak with sliced beans, and white wine and soda?

"Anything..." Sponer mumbled. The thought of food made him feel sick, but the waiter should bring something, no matter what; he then took his handkerchief from his breast pocket and wiped the sweat from his forehead. The waiter withdrew. Sponer stood up, felt himself swaying, stumbled towards a sofa, threw himself on it and closed his eyes.

He lay quite still.

He was no longer conscious of anything, he felt nothing, suddenly he was no longer afraid, he just lay there, his arms dangling lifelessly at his sides, and it felt good just to lie still. After a couple of minutes he even felt an edge of a cushion digging into the back of his neck. He turned over on his side and shut his eyes.

He felt completely indifferent to everything that happened or could still happen.

He might have been lying for about a quarter of an hour or even longer and perhaps been dozing off, when he again became aware of a noise. The waiter had opened the door and was now pushing a small food trolley into the room. Sponer sat up. The waiter, however, motioned to him that he should remain where he was, and that he would wheel the trolley up to the sofa.

"And how are you feeling now?" he asked.

At that moment the telephone rang.

Before Sponer's brain could latch on to what was happening, the waiter had walked to the telephone, lifted the receiver, spoken a few words, and was now passing Sponer the receiver, adding that the call was for him.

Sponer automatically put out his hand, but withdrew it immediately. The waiter, thinking that Sponer was too weak to come to the phone, tried to help him stand up. He actually helped Sponer to his feet and, before the latter could work out how to communicate to the waiter that he didn't want to take the call, the receiver was pressed into his hand, and the waiter stood by supporting him.

He heard a woman's voice speak in English at the other end of the line.

She first of all said a few words in the manner of a question, repeated the question after a moment, but in a different word order. Then, after a short pause, the voice became more urgent, fired a brief question a couple of times, and then uttered a fairly long sentence that Sponer understood just as little as the preceding questions.

After waiting a little, he put the phone down without answering. The waiter looked at him in astonishment.

"Wrong number," Sponer mumbled.

The waiter began serving food on a plate.

Sponer fell back again on the sofa.

"So!" he thought, but quite calmly. "So! Someone was phoning Mortimer." Now he'd have to consider the consequences. However, all of a sudden he could no longer think. His thoughts dissolved before him, they eluded him. Like a paper ball at the end of a string that is thrown to a kitten to play with and is then jerked back at the last moment, he found himself unable to grasp any of them. He stared despondently at the meat and vegetables in front of him, and ate only a meringue pie. The waiter mixed some white wine and soda, moved the table a little closer, bowed, and walked to the door. He had not reached it, however, when the phone rang for the second time.

The waiter was about to pick it up, but Sponer motioned him aside, as if to say, "Leave it! I'll get it myself." The waiter was already about to walk away, but when he saw Sponer still sitting motionless, he approached him again. The telephone continued to ring. Sponer got up. The waiter quickly moved the table away from the sofa, and left the room while Sponer was walking to the phone.

Sponer waited until the door had closed, then lifted the receiver. Again the woman's voice spoke in English.

While he was listening, Sponer tried to force himself to think what he should do next, but was unable to dispel the fog that still dulled his senses like a drug; or perhaps the events that had occurred in such rapid succession had exerted their full force on him in such a way that, whatever happened subsequently, they could no longer elicit a proper response from him, at least not for the moment. His nerves simply did not react any more. Even the new danger, this telephone conversation, could not make him decide what to do. The only thing he told himself was that if he so much as uttered a word, he was finished.

This time he didn't put the receiver down, but listened as in a trance to the increasingly rapid, imploring and finally threatening voice, which expected answers and received none, which shouted and pleaded for a response, and finally fell silent. He continued holding the receiver to his ear, and after about a minute put it down.

The voice, which at first was warm and soft like the caress of a hand, had finally risen in pitch to an anxious and shrill tone, tripping over itself; but then, just at the end, it called the name Jack several times in all the tones ranging from anger to anxiety and bewilderment. Sponer frowned as in exasperation. Was this the way they thought they could still get a response from Mortimer? No, not even a voice that shouted, threatened and implored in

93

such a manner would elicit an answer, and he, Sponer, kept silent like Mortimer.

For Mortimer's mouth was full of water, and was silent.

Sponer went to the table, took a few bites of food while standing, and finished off the wine. As he put down the glass, the phone rang again. He glanced at it fleetingly, lit a cigarette and took a couple of puffs. Now the smoke did him good. In the meantime the phone continued ringing at intervals.

At last he picked it up.

This time it was the receptionist. He said that a lady wanted to speak to Mr Mortimer. At first Sponer didn't fully comprehend. Where was the lady? he asked.

"Downstairs in the hall," the receptionist replied.

Sponer's heart again suddenly missed a beat. He couldn't come downstairs now! he stammered, and put the receiver down.

He took a couple of steps. The feeling of confusion that had afflicted him suddenly lifted, and was replaced by nervous anxiety. He was once more fully aware of his predicament.

He turned, lifted the receiver and, now himself, asked for the receptionist.

"Reception," he heard after a few seconds.

"Listen," Sponer said, "I don't want to speak to that lady now. Would you kindly make sure I'm not disturbed again. I'm not available to either that lady or anyone else who wants to speak to me. What on earth do you mean telling me that someone wants to speak to me in the middle of the night!

94

I don't want to take any calls from anyone! Please also tell the switchboard that there's no point in taking any calls for me. I'd be obliged if you wouldn't bother me any more!"

At that moment he heard the door being torn open behind his back, and he swung around.

A young, tall, slim platinum-blonde, very pretty, in an evening dress and a fur-trimmed brocade coat entered the room so quickly that when she walked towards him the hem of her dress rustled and swished round her ankles.

He stared at her and, still holding the receiver behind his back, groped around, missing the cradle each time, but finally he just let it drop anyhow.

# 6

JOSÉ MONTEMAYOR was a peon, a shepherd on horseback, in the wild south of the United States. He and the other vaqueros rounded up from the saddle huge herds of semi-wild cattle and horses on the vast plains of New Mexico, and when they chased the stampeding animals, the ends and fringes of their serapes, the colourful Indian shawls, fluttered behind them, and the prairie pollen and dust clouds of the llanos rose high into the sky. In high summer they stripped off their woollen shirts, tied them round their waists, and galloped bareback over the plains. Their hats, blown about by the strong wind, dangled from straps on their brown shoulders, and round their heads they wound coloured silk kerchiefs.

Small brass bells tingled on their saddles, lassos swayed back and forth, and the hairy strips of bearskin hanging from their stirrups fluttered in the wind. Montemayor also carried a guitar on his saddle. He had a good voice, and of an evening often sang songs to the others—old Spanish melodies and his own tunes that occurred to him from time to time.

Although he was only a cowboy, he was reputed to be the grandson of Lieutenant José Montemayor, who commanded the platoon that had shot Emperor Maximilian of Mexico.

One spring day, after collecting their pay, he and a couple of amigos set out on a spree, rode over the border, invaded all the Mexican taverns, flirted with the young women, spent their dollars and pesos on liquor, and generally painted the town red, finally ending up in Monterey, an old baroque hilltop town.

It was evening when they rode into the town, and the sun was setting like a fading rose behind the green copper cupolas and towers of Monterey. The streets, however, were already almost dark, the hooves clattered over the cobbles, the scent of jasmine wafted from the gardens in the twilight, the finery glinted on their saddles, and the women followed the riders with sparkling eyes.

They stopped in front of a tavern, tied up the horses, went in, and caroused into the night. They then left, and wandered through the town on foot.

The scent from the gardens became stronger, even overpowering the smell of cooking oil from the kitchen doorways and the other smells of a southern town. The full moon had long since risen and hung high in the silky blue of the night.

The peons wandered through the hushed streets, in which the only sound was the clinking of their silver spurs. The smoke of their cigarettes wafted behind them. Montemayor strode in front, strumming his guitar and singing, and the others sang along. Finally he started on a very old song which only he knew, while the others walked behind and listened, the only accompaniment being the strumming of the guitar and the clinking of spurs.

He had come to the end of a verse and was just about to begin the next when, from above a house cloaked in darkness, there came a woman's voice singing this very verse. It was a very beautiful, clear voice that floated in the moonlight. Montemayor stopped in his tracks, as did the others, and listened in amazement, accompanying the unfamiliar singer on his guitar. He couldn't see where the voice was coming from. He was just about to peer into the shadows that enveloped the house when the moon, gliding over the roof with the curved tiles which glistened like white breakers, shone straight in his face, but not before he had made out the outlines of a roof garden or a sort of elevated, enclosed arbour, from which he realized the voice was issuing.

The song consisted of alternate question and answer verses. The questions were to be sung by a male, the answers, by a female voice; when the invisible singer had come to the end of the maiden's verse, Montemayor continued singing the man's part, then came the maiden's turn, then the man's voice again, followed by the maiden's, and so on.

It was the final verse, and whereas the voice of the invisible singer had, to begin with, sounded shy, timid and reserved, it now changed to an expression of fervour and affection.

The voice then fell silent. After a moment's pause during which they savoured the magic sounds that had now ceased, the peons broke into applause. Montemayor then stepped forward and, taking off his hat with a flourish and holding it in his lowered hand so that the tassels touched the ground, enquired whether the best singer in the south would do him and his comrades the honour of showing herself.

The figure of a woman or girl, silhouetted in the light of the moon shining through the veil on her head, appeared in the arbour above.

The other peons, too, now took off their hats, their tassels and straps touching the ground.

"Who are you?" the girl asked, though since she was Spanish, she actually put it in the Spanish manner: "Whom do I have the honour of addressing?"

"We are," Montemayor answered, "cowboys and peons from the States, who've ridden across the border to meet the beauties of Mexico. Would you honour us by revealing your name, so that when we return home we can tell everyone what the most beautiful of them all is called."

The young woman laughed. "My name is Consuelo," she said. "And when you return, you can tell your people that in fact you never even saw me. I can see you clearly in the moonlight, but I have the moon behind me. It makes it easier for you to imagine that I'm the most beautiful."

"We don't need the moon," one of the group shouted, "to know that you must be as enchanting as your voice!"

"You flatter me too much," the young woman said. "In fact, my voice is nothing special, I hardly use it, and my mother, who also taught me the few songs that I know, sang much better than I do. I must go now! The people in the house are already asleep, and it's not right for me to carry on talking to such charming young people as yourselves."

This was Spanish courtesy, a matter of etiquette in response to the compliments that had been paid her. However, it was more than courtesy, for she added, "Especially to the singer among you."

This was a direct reference, which they understood immediately.

"We wouldn't want to cause you any trouble!" the one who'd just spoken said, after looking at Montemayor. "We're going now and we wish you a good night. However, we should be honoured if you would give us something to remember you by."

"With pleasure," the young woman said. She plucked a flower from the arbour. "And now, adios," she said, and threw the flower to Montemayor.

He caught it and kissed it.

The peons bowed. "Adios!" they shouted.

"Adios!" the maiden replied, and waved farewell to them.

They broke into a new song and returned to their inn. The sound of their singing and spurs echoed in the narrow street. In front of the tavern they untied the blankets from their saddles, went inside, rolled themselves in the blankets, and went to sleep. Montemayor, however, remained standing by the door and smoked a cigarette. He then threw it away and returned to Consuelo.

She was still leaning against an arch of the arbour when he appeared in the street below. He stepped into the shadow of the house, pulled himself up by the window grating, grabbed hold of the railing of the arbour and swung himself up.

Bent thus over the railing, he now began to woo her. Her parents were simple people, but she behaved as if she were a high-born lady. The moon had already been waning for a long time before she finally permitted Montemayor to kiss her hands. The pale light fell sideways upon her face. Until then he had seen it only in the half-light in which her eyes sparkled, but now he saw for the first time how beautiful she was. The moon had by now almost disappeared, and dawn had nearly broken, and still she listened to Montemayor.

The following day the peons left the town, but Montemayor followed them only several days later, and when he left it was only to return. He returned almost every month to Monterey.

The following year there was an outbreak of cattle-plague that destroyed huge herds, and he lost his job. He used up all his savings in search of new work and was forced to sing with his guitar in taverns and small hotels in order to survive; for this he was given accommodation and occasionally meals, and also some of the audience would invite him to their table and ply him with drinks. Finally the director of a travelling cabaret troupe engaged him. He was successful everywhere in the small towns where he appeared, though without a partner such a singer could not make a mark. It was suggested to him that he should look around for a partner. He got on a train and travelled the stretch that he'd so often ridden on horseback, to Monterey.

He proposed to Consuelo that she became his partner, which she decided to do, not so much because she thought she could make a go of it, but rather because she loved Montemayor. But fortune smiled on them, they were a great success, mainly, of course, on account of Consuelo's beauty. Montemayor's own forte lay in fact not so much in the singing itself, but rather in his talent for arranging old songs. After their latest engagement in Palm Beach, they went to New York.

Montemayor was by then beginning to publish songs, yet he lacked that extra something to produce a hit. He realized that he'd have to study classical music in order to be able to compose popular music. Their nightly appearances still remained his and Consuelo's main source of income. He played the guitar and Consuelo danced and sang in Spanish costume with a foot-high comb in her hair. They earned money, he wore good suits, and Consuelo had a selection of pretty dresses. Also, he gave her jewellery, but in truth these were only small trinkets.

Yet he loved Consuelo so much that he was quite happy to see her reap more success than came his way. His own talent hardly amounted to anything. Moreover, when all was said and done, he still remained the peon that he'd always been; he gave a little of his soul and passion to his music, all the rest belonged to his beloved. If he hadn't had Consuelo, he'd have been very unhappy. The fact was, he felt out of place in a city. He often dreamt of the prairies. However, a woman never hankers after the past. Consuelo was successful, she was acclaimed; she gave a little of her soul and passion to Montemayor, the rest went to her new way of life.

One evening she received a visiting card via her manager; a certain Jack Mortimer invited her to come to his house after the performance and sing to his guests. This Jack Mortimer, added the manager in case she didn't know, was the son of Mortimer, the banker. Yes, she knew that, said Consuelo; and the manager mentioned a very high fee.

Montemayor, of course, didn't know who Mortimer was. Both he and Consuelo were well received in Mortimer's house, and from the start were treated as equals with the guests, comprising a group young people of the wealthy set and some strikingly pretty young women and wives. Mortimer about that time would have been about twenty-three or -four. He was utterly captivated by Montemayor's and Consuelo's singing.

They sat down to a table that was groaning with food and drink. Some of those present began, in the traditional American way, to get plastered as quickly as possible and then slump around on sofas. Mortimer gave a dismissive wave of his hand. It was good, he said, that they'd got rid of them—now they'd have some peace and quiet; and then he asked Consuelo to sing.

Sitting at the table, Consuelo and Montemayor sang a song, and those present showered them with applause, and yet the conversation immediately turned to other topics and the singing was forgotten. Mortimer finally got up and announced that he'd be more than happy if people wanted to wander round and take a look at his house. The guests dispersed in small groups in the spacious abode.

When they all reassembled, Consuelo and Mortimer were missing. The twenty minutes that elapsed before the two finally appeared were almost as painful and embarrassing to the company as to Montemayor himself. Where had they been? Just simply not there. All the time they were away, it seemed as if they were deliberately trying to humiliate someone, and when they finally appeared, Consuelo acted as if nothing had happened, while Mortimer didn't even try to conceal his pleasure.

The period that followed became for Montemayor one of unbearable anguish. Spurred on by personal vanity, it is quite easy to fight for the constancy of a woman whom one hardly loves any more. But it is impossible to hold on to a woman with whom one is still in love and who does not requite that love. Montemayor was leaving behind a trail of blood from his heart, which had been mortally wounded not by Mortimer but by Consuelo herself. She disarmed him by not making any secret of the fact that she no longer loved him. Jealousy can only exist when one hopes one has made a mistake. With her indifference, however, Consuelo convinced him that he had not made a mistake. He remonstrated with her, of course, but she did not react. He no longer had any claim to her heart.

If he'd still been in his own country, he'd have known what to do. There a woman is not free. She belongs to him who can defend her. Here, however, she was free. She could do whatever she wanted. In the States no man any longer has a natural right to a woman. She no longer needs his protection, she does what she wants. Mortimer, too, told him that. Montemayor had drawn him into an argument in order, at the end of it, to beat the daylights out of him.

However, Mortimer said, "I haven't a clue what you want. You think Consuelo loves me? I believe you're mistaken. One doesn't fall in love so quickly. There's too much else going on. Naturally, I was flattered to see Consuelo here and there, but I'm pretty sure she's not really interested in me. She wants to make a career. You shouldn't stand in her way. I myself have done what I can for her. Hasn't she said anything to you about that? I've introduced her to many people who could be useful to her. Honestly, you're wrong if you think I've got any ulterior motives. I was only a middleman. I haven't even seen Consuelo for the last two or three days. However, I introduced her to George Anstruther. Do you know Anstruther? You don't? Well, he's extremely influential. They say he's very interested in Consuelo. Malicious gossips even say she's his mistress."

Having said that, Mortimer lit a cigarette. Montemayor looked him in the eyes for a moment, turned short on his heel and left.

Lately he had seen Consuelo only in the evenings when they performed together. He returned to his flat, packed a few things, and left New York without even seeing Consuelo or even so much as contacting his manager. The intermezzo was at an end. He would, he decided, become a peon once more, and that was that.

Two days later he got off the train in a small station in the South. It was raining. The rain was falling in sheets over the prairie, drumming on the tin roof of the station, forming puddles between the tracks. On the horizon a couple clapboard houses appeared to be sinking in a sea of mud.

He stared into the wilderness. A pair of horses saddled the Mexican way stood at the corner of a house, their shanks turned towards the weather. The tall grass swayed, the rain beat down, the gloom and the mist were closing in.

He enquired when the next train was due.

He had two hours to wait. He didn't wait under the station canopy, but stood out in the open. His shoes, his coat, his business suit were soaking wet.

The sound of singing, shouting and laughter reached him from the house where the horses were tied up.

No one bothered about him.

At last the train came. It was heading for New Orleans.

In New Orleans he had to wait a day. He sailed on the *Jeanne d'Arc* to France.

In Paris he appeared on the stage with several artistes, whom he often changed. Day in, day out, he studied music. After a year he moved to Berlin, then back to Paris again.

He got people to write French and English lyrics to his melodies, and published them.

'Juanita' made him famous.

He returned to the States; however, he stayed only a short time in New York, travelled down to the South again, and bought a property in Florida near Palm Beach.

Here he composed his second great hit, 'Castilliana'.

He made several hundred thousand dollars from this hit. He wrote the song one evening very quickly, in a matter of minutes, before driving to Palm Beach to meet some friends, and the moon over the sea was just like it had been that time over Monterey.

'Castilliana' was played endlessly at parties where people first danced and then the women went and deceived their husbands.

From now on he lived part of the time in Palm Beach and

part of the time in New York and Paris. The much heralded 'Sonora' was a flop.

In New York he learnt that Mortimer no longer lived there, but had moved to Chicago, where he ran his father's bank.

He didn't enquire after Consuelo, and people obviously avoided mentioning her name in his presence. No one knew whether he still thought about her. Also, her name no longer appeared anywhere. He couldn't find her on any programme or notice.

One day he got to know George Anstruther. He was a very handsome man of about forty. They obviously didn't talk about Consuelo. Strangely enough, though, Montemayor let slip a few words about Jack Mortimer. Anstruther smiled in a peculiar way. This was like a red rag to a bull, and Anstruther, in order not to be misinterpreted, felt obliged to justify himself why he had reacted that way: wasn't Montemayor aware that Mortimer... "Go on!" Montemayor shouted, his heart missing a beat... that Mortimer, said Anstruther, was now more of a gangster than a banker, like so many other bankers, judges and businessmen in the States. "I see," Montemayor mumbled, and they talked a little bit more about Mortimer's possible connections with the underworld, and then about other things. It became clear to Montemayor that Mortimer's bank was in financial difficulties; however, it was not uncommon even for wealthy people to get mixed up with criminals in the end.

A few days later Montemayor learnt by chance from people

who knew nothing of his sad tale, that Consuelo had been suffering from tuberculosis and had died in a sanatorium in the Rocky Mountains some three years previously.

Two months later he married Winifred Parr.

Late that autumn Montemayor travelled with Winifred to Paris. One evening after the opera, when they were having supper at Ciro's, Montemayor noticed Winifred nod at someone who was sitting behind him, evidently to acknowledge a greeting. He turned around; it was Jack Mortimer.

Mortimer immediately came over to their table. He knew Winifred fleetingly from earlier times. He spoke a few inconsequential words and behaved as though nothing had ever happened between himself and Montemayor.

Before Montemayor could stop her, Winifred had invited him to join them.

What followed in the next few days was quite inevitable. Mortimer had never shown any particular interest in Winifred. However, when he saw that she was Montemayor's wife, he immediately became excited.

People who've already once deprived a man of his wife will feel almost compelled to do it a second time.

Montemayor himself immediately sensed that in Mortimer's eyes it wasn't Winifred, but in actual fact Consuelo who was sitting next to Montemayor. The only difference was that he didn't love Winifred half as much as he had loved Consuelo.

It became at once clear that he'd be able to protect her better than his previous love.

Winifred knew nothing of Consuelo, but she immediately sensed the tension between the two men, and she reacted as any pretty but empty-headed woman would in such a situation. Straight away she enjoyed to the full the interest that Mortimer was showing in her. Had Montemayor ignored Mortimer, she'd have done the same. However, since she noticed Montemayor's jealousy, there was no greater pleasure for her than to fall in love with Mortimer.

At this stage, of course, it would still have been easy for Montemayor to have dashed the hopes that the two were entertaining. He could simply have gone away somewhere with Winifred, and that would have been the end of the matter. However, after his initial aversion, it occurred to him that Mortimer's presence was right up his street. He still had a score to settle with Mortimer. An opportunity now arose for Montemayor to make out that he couldn't care less about Mortimer's advances. He'd be able to play with Winifred like a puppet on a string.

Truly, what was the struggle for Winifred compared to the struggle for Consuelo? Nothing. Pure vanity. Montemayor had no illusions about this. But the easier it appeared to him to defend Winifred, the more heartbroken he felt that he'd lost his Consuelo. He had almost forgotten Mortimer, but now he began to hate him again vehemently.

All this, however, robbed Montemayor of his peace of

mind. He never left Winifred's side day and night, which made Mortimer, who always tagged along, look ridiculous. The only thing was that he began to have misgivings about himself, to such an extent that finally he began to hate the very sight of Mortimer. He couldn't help reliving the old tragedy whenever he saw the man, and he began to drool over Winifred, for whom, when all was said and done, he couldn't give a fig, just as much as he had drooled over Consuelo, whom he had worshipped.

Meanwhile, his opposition drove the two lovers ever closer together. They understood each other without so much as exchanging a word. In the end they really fell in love. They could read this in each other's eyes, they passed secret notes between themselves, they spoke in a sort of code which they alone could decipher. Montemayor was aware of this, but he lost his nerve and finally decided to depart. He accepted one of the contracts that people were forever offering him, and told Winifred that in two days' time they'd be going to Vienna, where he was to give a jazz concert.

These two days were sufficient for Mortimer to arrange with Winifred that he'd come on after her, stay in hiding in Vienna and meet up with her there. Montemayor's decision to leave suited them even more than the present, unsatisfactory arrangement. They believed that Montemayor would not suspect Mortimer, who had business to conduct in Paris, of following them to Vienna, and would give his wife all the freedom that she'd enjoyed previously.

They were mistaken. Montemayor was prepared for this eventuality. True, he wasn't able to establish anything definite, but all the same he guessed what they were up to. It was obvious enough.

He travelled with Winifred and booked in at the Imperial. He told himself that there'd be no sense in intercepting Winifred's mail, since Mortimer would hardly risk writing to her at the hotel. Although he and Winifred for the most part went out together, when he was at rehearsals, he had to leave her on her own. He didn't doubt for a moment that she'd use that opportunity to collect the letters which Mortimer had sent her. If they were poste restante, she'd need her passport to claim them. He couldn't very well take that; however, he was in possession of her other documents, and, with the help of their marriage certificate, every time he left the hotel for any length of time he enquired at the post office if there were letters for Winifred Montemayor. He might have missed the odd one; at last, however, just as he was about to go to a rehearsal, a page boy, whom he'd drawn into his confidence, brought him secretly, as instructed, a telegram from Mortimer to Winifred. He was coming the next day at half past six in the evening, and was staying at the Bristol. She should give him a ring there at the first opportunity.

He destroyed this message and went to the rehearsal. The following day he left Winifred completely to her own devices till the evening. Come the evening, however, her nervousness indicated to him that, even though that particular telegram had not reached her, she must have been informed of Mortimer's arrival in some other way. Shortly before seven she found an opportunity to ring the Bristol. Mortimer, she was told, had booked in, but hadn't arrived yet. From then on she had no more opportunity to call him till midnight. Montemayor did not leave her side. They went to the opera, had supper, and sat for a while in the hotel bar. Towards midnight, when she feared she'd be unable to conceal the state of her nerves any longer, she said she was going to bed.

He took her upstairs. They occupied a two-bedroom suite, separated by a sitting room. She wished him good night in the sitting room, then Winifred went into her bedroom and Montemayor into his; however, he stopped at the door and listened.

A few minutes later he heard Winifred open her door softly, presumably to see if anyone was in the sitting room. Then she closed it. Montemayor immediately opened his, darted into the sitting room and listened at Winifred's door.

He heard her making a telephone call in a hushed voice and ask for Mortimer. Though she spoke a few words, it seemed she had got the wrong number, because she immediately rang again. Now she spoke for longer, her voice getting louder and more urgent; finally she put the receiver down and then rang once again, this time the reception at the Bristol. Then she rang off.

Montemayor at once stepped back from the door and got back to his room, not a moment too soon because he now heard Winifred enter the sitting room, lock her door, remove the key and go out.

Montemayor, hatless and without his overcoat, followed her immediately. She ran down the stairs. Once or twice she turned around, but he managed to conceal himself in the nick of time behind a corner or a pillar so that she didn't notice him. She left the hotel, as did he, too, a couple of moments later. He saw her rush across the street, her brocade opera cloak shimmering in the light of the street lamps. It was only about a couple of hundred yards to the Bristol. She went in, and through the glass door Montemayor saw her talking to the hall porter. Then the porter made a telephone call. In the meantime she ran up the stairs. The porter, it seemed, made as if to hold her back; he called something out, but she had already disappeared behind a bend on the stairs. The next moment Montemayor also entered and ran up the stairs. He saw Winifred run along the corridor of the first floor, open a door and disappear inside; he, too, rushed towards the door.

Winifred closed the door behind her, found herself standing in a lobby, opened the next door and stood in Mortimer's salon.

She was so ill prepared for the person she was rushing towards not to be Jack Mortimer that she discovered this only when she was nearly on top of him. She stopped dead with

114

a light shriek, held up her hand, sparkling with rings, to her mouth, half agape with horror, and stared at Sponer with ever widening, blazing eyes, without uttering a single word.

Sponer, too, still leaning against the mirror stand which held the telephone looked at her in motionless silence.

Finally, she mumbled something in English, probably an apology that she'd entered the wrong room, turned around and made to rush out through the door.

She had, however, barely taken a couple of steps when her eyes lit on the things that Sponer had pulled out of Mortimer's suitcases and that were now strewn all over the place.

She hesitated, seemed to recognize them, turned round again, the cloak slid off her shoulders, and the expression in her wide-open eyes, showed that she understood everything.

She stood there stock-still for two more seconds, only that the expression of fear intensified ever more, then she let out a cry which rose in pitch, swung around and dashed towards the door.

But in two bounds Sponer was already in front of her and had barred her way. She wanted to push him aside, but, slamming the door with his left hand, he grabbed her by the shoulder with his right. He flung her on the sofa and, through clenched teeth and with an almost demented look in his eyes, hissed, "You so much as cry out or try to get away and I'll knock you into next week!"

# 7

F ROM THE FORCE with which he flung her down and her overwhelming sense of fear, she lay there crouching, staring at him in utter bewilderment. Also, possibly she hadn't understood what he had said. Yet she guessed well enough, for initially she remained subdued and then finally made a movement as if to jump up, but fell back when she saw his expression, but only in order immediately to straighten herself up and cry out:

"Where's Jack Mortimer?"

"Shut up!" he hissed, then he listened whether anyone in the corridor or in the adjacent rooms had been alerted by the shouting and slamming of the door. But everything was quiet. The woman, too, was now silent, only panic flickered in her eyes. He approached her slowly; she shrank back again. He stood in front of her and, staring down at her, formulated in his mind a few words to say in English.

"How did you get here?" he asked finally.

"Where's Mortimer?" she mumbled again.

He gestured with his hand.

"Answer me!" he barked. "How did you get here? Were you the person who phoned earlier?"

She appeared not to understand him. He began to think that perhaps he hadn't expressed himself clearly enough. At school he'd learnt English, but only for a fairly short time, and very superficially. He repeated slowly and clearly: "Did you phone earlier?"

"Yes," she answered finally. "Who are you? Where's Mortimer?" And she began once more, getting ever louder, to speak so quickly that he no longer understood her. With a flick of his hand he cut her short. She fell silent; only her eyes continued to flicker.

"I can't tell you where Mortimer is," he said.

"Why not?" she retorted. "How come you're in his room? Why are his things lying about here?"

And she repeated her question when she noticed that he understood her poorly, and also added a few more.

"Can't you speak German?" he asked. But when he realized that she hadn't understood him, he said in English, "I've several things to ask you. When you answer, don't say so much and"—at this point he didn't know how to say "above all"—"not so quickly. Otherwise I won't understand you. Who was…"—here he corrected himself—"Who is this Jack Mortimer?"

She replied with a question that he didn't understand.

"I want to know," he insisted, "who Jack Mortimer is."

"Surely you must know that yourself!" she shouted. "You must!"

"No," he said, "I don't."

She looked around wildly, was about to answer, but then merely pointed at Mortimer's things.

"No," he said. "Even so, I don't know. But you're going to tell me." He thought for a moment, then took the letters from the table and held them out to her.

She immediately snatched at them and glanced at him in horror.

"Are these your letters?" he asked.

She didn't answer.

"Are these your letters?" he repeated. "Was he a friend of yours?"

She stayed silent and clutched the letters tightly in her hand.

"Was he a friend of yours?" he insisted. "Answer me!"

She broke into tears.

He turned away. The appearance of this woman had made his situation utterly intolerable. When he turned and looked at her again, the expression in her eyes was one of fury and unmitigated hatred.

"It's not my fault," he said, "that I'm now here instead of Mortimer. Believe me!"

Her eyes continued to flicker in hatred.

"It's not my fault," he repeated. "Do you understand?"

She remained silent.

He shrugged his shoulders.

"Where did Jack Mortimer come from?" he asked finally.

He had to repeat the question twice before she answered, "From Paris."

"And how," he asked, "do you know him? Have you known him long?"

She didn't reply.

"Listen," he said, slowly searching for the right words, "you have to answer what I ask you!"

"You know it all yourself!" she retorted.

"No," he said, "I told you already that I don't, but you're going to tell me. If not, I'm going to"—he searched for the right words for a moment—"make you. I'm sorry, but I've got to make you speak."

He wanted to add that his position left him no choice, but this proved too difficult to translate. He reached for her hands and squeezed them together till she let out a cry.

"I'm sorry," he repeated, and took a step back.

She again began to cry. He wished he hadn't hurt her, and wanted to stroke her hair. She immediately flared up and lashed out at his hand. He shrugged his shoulders.

"So, I want an answer," he said curtly. "Who are you?"

She clenched her teeth.

"What's your name?" he repeated.

"None of your business!" she shouted. "I didn't want to come to you. You've no right to ask my name!"

"Too bad," he said. "You've got to tell me who you are!"

"No!"

"Yes," he said, and reached for her hands again. She snatched them away.

"Well, what's your name?" he asked.

119

"Jane," she hissed.

He thought for a moment. Then he suddenly grabbed the letters out of her hand, flipped through them even though she was trying to snatch them back, found the one he wanted, and showed her the letter W.

She blushed to the roots of her hair.

"Well?" he asked.

"That's my surname," she mumbled. "I'm Jane Ward."

"Since when," he wanted to ask, "have people signed love letters with their surnames?" But again he couldn't translate it. Looking hard at her, he pointedly touched with the tip of his shoe her evening bag, which was lying on the floor. Then he picked it up. She thought he was going to give it to her but he only pointed at the metal monogram, a W and an M.

She reddened even more, couldn't think of anything to say, and merely tried to grab the bag. However, he drew it out of her reach, opened it hastily, saw a couple of letters inside and pulled them out. They were addressed to Mrs Winifred Montemayor: one to Vienna, the Hotel Imperial; the other was poste restante. Then he let her have the letters and the bag.

He had gained the upper hand. In the course of the next few minutes, while she was in a state of confusion and seeing that she had the bag in her possession so that she could wipe away her tearstains and powder her nose, he managed to drag her story out of her.

The name Montemayor was, of course, familiar to him.

He even remembered having heard a couple of his records. He also questioned her about Mortimer. Only there wasn't much she could tell him, except that he was the son of a banker and that she had known him fleetingly and had then met him in Paris once more.

Suddenly he realized that she was at his feet. She had slid down from the sofa, was clinging to him and imploring him to tell her where Mortimer was.

"Did you love him a lot?" he mumbled.

Then his eyes wandered round the room. He saw the two cigarette packets: Mortimer's on the settee; and the second one, which the waiter had brought up, on the dining table.

He extricated himself from Winifred's grip and went over to get himself a cigarette.

He hadn't reached the table when a sound made him look around.

Winifred had jumped to her feet, run to the door, had flung it open and was now running through the lobby towards the exit door.

Before he could take even one step in pursuit, she had torn the exit door open and was about to run out, but instead let out an almighty cry and staggered back. A man in an evening suit came in. He banged the door shut after him and clapped his hand on her mouth to stifle the cry. She struggled for air. He grabbed her with his other, free hand and dragged her into the salon. His face was so distorted with rage, the likes of which Sponer had not seen before.

He glanced around, appeared not to notice Sponer at all, and dragged Winifred over to one of the windows. There he reached behind the curtains and yanked one of the curtains cords with such force that the whole rail came crashing down. He folded the rope double and began to lash the woman with it.

So far he hadn't said a word; now, however, he began to accompany every word with a suppressed expletive. Under the blows Winifred's thin evening dress immediately tore into shreds and red welts began to appear on her naked back. At first, when she had got her mouth free, she began to yell; however, the blows came down so thick and fast that she immediately found herself short of breath. She hid her face in her arms, stopped turning around and just groaned. The man continued to whip her.

At first Sponer observed the scene in bewilderment till his mind slowly began to comprehend what was going on. Above all he didn't know what to make of the intruder. He now grabbed him by the shoulders, yelled at him and pushed him aside. Since the fellow nevertheless paid not the slightest attention to him and carried on lashing blindly, even catching him once or twice with the ends of the swishing rope, Sponer spun him round and with his clenched fist hit him square in the face.

The man went down immediately and the woman, too, whom he let go, fell down and lay there whimpering.

*

A couple of moments later the man began to move again, pressed his hand to his cheek, straightened himself up unsteadily and took two or three shaky steps towards Sponer.

Sponer recoiled and was ready to confront him again. However, this attack amounted to no more than that the man, in coming forward, lost his balance and merely tumbled into Sponer's arms. Sponer pushed him away. The man took a couple of steps back, pulled out a handkerchief, pressed it to the spot where the punch had landed, and also felt his chin and the rest of his face while he eyed Sponer. Then he shook his head as though he wanted to shake something off; he began to sway again, but managed to hold onto the edge of the table. Sponer was ready to support him. The man, leaning on the table, looked at Sponer. "Who are you?" he asked.

Meanwhile Winifred had sat up, groaning, had pulled the tatters of her evening gown round her shoulders and was groping her way to the sofa. Sponer picked up the brocade cloak from the floor, approached her and threw it over her shoulders.

"Why did you hit her?" he asked the man.

"Because," the man hissed, "she is my wife!"

"Are you Montemayor?"

"Yes." He turned to face Winifred again and, leaning on the backrest, took a couple of steps towards her. "What did you want here?" he said in a cracked voice. "Didn't you want to get to Mortimer?"

She shrank back even more as he approached. Sponer pushed him back.

"Leave her alone now," he ordered. "How did you get here in the first place? How did you know your wife was here?"

"Because I heard her telephone just a while ago. Did you think," he said, turning to Winifred, "I was asleep already? Didn't it occur to you, I'd be expecting you to get in touch with that man?"

"What man?" she cried.

"Mortimer!"

"Where is Mortimer?"

"'Where is Mortimer?' she asks me!"

"Yes! He's not here! He's gone! Instead there's this man here," and she pointed at Sponer. Montemayor turned to Sponer; however, the woman went on to speak so quickly that Sponer could no longer understand her, nor the man when he answered. After that, the woman rattled on and cried ever louder, then she finally felt silent; only, her eyes kept darting from Montemayor to Sponer and back again.

Montemayor looked at Sponer.

"Are you Austrian?" he asked.

"Yes," Sponer said after a pause.

"My wife," Montemayor said in broken German, "says this is Mortimer's room and these," he pointed at the things scattered about, "are his clothes. Which they are. I know them from Paris, where he was wearing them. Where is Mortimer? How come you're here?"

Sponer was silent for a moment, then he asked, "How is it that you speak German?"

"I studied music here."

"In Vienna?"

"No, in Germany. So, who are you?"

"And you followed," Sponer interrupted him, "your wife when you heard that she had phoned Mortimer?"

"Yes."

"You said you suspected your wife would ring Jack Mortimer. What made you suspect that?"

"Because," Montemayor replied, "even in Paris…"—and he turned to Winifred and shouted in English again—"Because even in Paris she wanted to get together with him, and because she, when we were coming here, had arranged that he'd follow. I knew all about it, I wasn't born yesterday! And they wanted to meet here!"

Winifred glanced at him with an indescribable look on her face. "Why then," she interrupted, "did you have to hit me if I wasn't with Mortimer at all?"

"Because," he yelled, "you wanted to be with him! Or maybe you didn't want to be with him after all? Is he the one," he said, pointing at Sponer, "you wanted to be with? How do you know him anyway?"

"I don't know him at all! He was here when I came in, but he won't say where Mortimer is!"

Montemayor looked at Sponer. "Well?" he asked. "Where is he?"

Sponer did not reply. Since these two, who knew Mortimer, had found him here, it made no sense to continue publicly playing Mortimer's part to the end. It was madness to have taken it on in the first place. Because, in spite of all that he'd done, he had achieved nothing except to incriminate himself hopelessly and let the real murderer go absolutely scot-free.

He shrugged his shoulders, glanced around, went over to the table, took a cigarette and headed for the door.

Winifred sat up on the sofa, leapt to her feet, ran after Sponer and held him back by his arm.

"Where are you going?" she cried.

He looked at her, and a look of hatred came into his eyes. If it hadn't been for this woman, he thought, if it hadn't been for her obsession to see Mortimer, it might perhaps have been possible to fake the departure the next morning, to leave the hotel, take a cab, disappear, save himself. As it was, she had deceived her husband, saved the one who had shot her lover and ruined him, Sponer.

He turned to go.

"Where are you off to?" she cried.

He freed himself from her with a jerk. He looked at her pretty, vacuous face, staring back at him at close quarters; there was no other expression except obsession for the man with whom she wanted to double-cross her husband. Uncontrollable anger welled up in him. Had he been able to destroy her with the words he yelled into her face, he'd gladly have done so.

"Mortimer," he yelled at her, "is dead!"

She collapsed straight away. While Montemayor, after a momentary shock, lifted her up and carried her to the sofa, Sponer went back to the table, filled a glass with water, dipped a napkin in it, and handed the napkin to Montemayor. Montemayor pressed it to her forehead. A few seconds later she came to and began to sob desperately, mumble something and cry out the same question over and over again. She was in total shock.

At last she buried her face in her hands and grew calmer, only now and again her whole body would convulse with a shudder.

Leaning against the table, Sponer looked at her closely.

"Listen," he said finally, "I didn't do it. I'm a taxi driver, my name's Ferdinand Sponer. I'd never seen Mortimer until he got into my cab tonight. When I reached the Opera House, he was dead. I don't know who shot him. I saw so little of what had happened that I said to myself, 'If I'm unable to give any evidence, I'll be taken for the murderer.' I wanted to play Mortimer's role to avoid being suspected myself. All I've achieved as a result is that I'll be taken for the murderer. I can't disprove it. You can report me. If you do that, however, you'll ensure that the real murderer is never found."

While he spoke, she had raised her head again and was staring at him wild-eyed. She couldn't understand what he was saying. Montemayor interpreted it for her in a few words.

"You," she shouted at Sponer, "killed Mortimer yourself!"

Sponer shrugged his shoulders. "Whatever for?" he asked. "I didn't know him from Adam. All I know is what you told me. Do you think I did it because of his money? He hardly had any on him." He took Mortimer's wallet from the table, pulled out the cheque book and the little money that it contained, and threw them down. "There!" he said. "Or do you think it was because of his things? He only had these two suitcases and a few odds and ends on him." He produced Mortimer's passport and the Colt revolver, and also chucked them down, followed by the silver and a couple of cartridges. "That's the lot," he said. "Hardly worth killing for, is it? I didn't do it, but neither do I know who might have done it."

Winifred glanced at the things with horror, and Montemayor looked at them, too.

"Perhaps," Montemayor said, "his fate just caught up with him."

"What fate?" Sponer asked.

"He was," said Montemayor, "after all, a gangster."

"What was he?"

"A gangster, a criminal."

"Who? Mortimer?"

"It's not true!" Winifred cried.

"Yes, it is!" Montemayor shouted back. "He was every inch a gangster! His whole character proved it! His success with women proved it! The way in which he chased after

you, and the way you reacted to him proved it! You knew
that yourself anyway!"

"Me?"

"Yes, you! It was George Anstruther himself who told
me that!"

"What did he tell you?"

"Everyone knows about it there!"

"A man of his wealth wouldn't…"

"He had none any more! He was through! And if he
wasn't a criminal himself, he lived off the crimes of others!
He sold stolen stocks and shares, he was in cahoots with
crooks and I don't know what else! He was in no danger of
getting into trouble with the police, that's for sure! Whom
do the police go after over there do you think? Gangsters?
They wouldn't dare. But he did seem to run the risk of
getting into trouble with his own kind, the crooks. Let's
face it, it's the gangsters themselves who bump off one
another, isn't it?"

"Here in Europe? You must be mad!"

"No, not at all! He was gunned down. They saw a chance
and took it. It wouldn't even occur to the local police, who
are quite ignorant of such things, to make the connection."

"And who would have done it?"

"One of their own. Every so often they come over here,
too; the world's their oyster. And the art is to do it in a
moving car! To hop on, fire, hop off without even the driver
noticing, and…"

"He must have noticed it! You heard the shot, didn't you?" she yelled at Sponer.

"There were three," Sponer said coldly. "One in the throat, two in the chest."

She was about to say something, but couldn't. "And where," she muttered at last, "is he now?"

"Mortimer?" he asked.

"Yes."

He made a vague gesture.

"Where is he?" she yelled.

"Do you want to see him?" he asked. "You won't be able to. No one will see him again." He lit a cigarette and gave the woman who had ruined his life a cold, hard look.

"What do you mean?" she mumbled. "Where is he?"

"In the river," he said. "The river's long. It'll take him some time to get to the sea. How should I know where Mortimer is now!"

She let out a cry, jumped up from the sofa, clenched her fists and pounced on him. He looked at her coldly without defending himself or trying to restrain her. The woman's mortification was the dead man's only revenge. But how long, Sponer thought to himself, is this going to go on for? I shall probably never taste freedom again. Whereas she?… In a few months, perhaps in a few weeks, she'll go on deceiving her husband with another man, just as she did with Jack Mortimer.

He grabbed her wrists and shoved her away in exasperation.

She tumbled backwards, was about to say something, but swung around suddenly, rushed to the phone and grabbed the receiver. Montemayor was immediately at her side.

"What are you up to now?" he asked.

"Get the police!" she snapped.

"You'll do nothing of the sort," he said. However, she paid no attention to him whatever, lifted the receiver and had already opened her mouth to ask for connection when he snatched the receiver out of her hand.

"Leave it alone!" he commanded, and rang off.

"I wouldn't dream of it!" she cried, and reached for the phone again.

He held the receiver firmly. "Stop it!" he cried.

"What's come over you?" she shouted.

"You're not going to phone!"

"Why not?"

"Because I, your husband, forbid you!"

"You're no longer my husband, and there's nothing you can forbid me!"

"Ah!" he exclaimed. "Is that so? Maybe because you wanted to double-cross me, is that it?"

"Yes."

"Only you haven't done it! Sure, you wanted to do it, but it didn't quite work out, did it?"

"Let me phone!"

"No!"

"You no longer own me! I was already unfaithful to you in Paris!"

He laughed. "Really?" he said. "Do you think Mortimer would still have followed you here after that? It wouldn't even have entered his head, I tell you. He wasn't that type. Do you imagine he loved you? He didn't love you. He only wanted to use you to hurt me, that's all!"

"That's a lie!" she shouted.

"I knew him better than you."

"No, that's not true! But even if it were, I'd still love him and hate you, because I can't live with you any more!"

"You'll just have to get used to it. You're not a free agent. You haven't been unfaithful to me and, rest assured, you won't! Nor will I allow you to compromise yourself by contacting the police! No one need know that you've been here!"

"Not even the police?"

"Yes, that's right. Because they're just not going to know."

"Why not?"

"Because you're not going to report it to them!"

"You think you can stop me?"

"Yes."

"No, you can't!"

"You'll be surprised! And I shan't go to the police either. Because my reputation is worth more to me than yours and all this sordid murder of your lover. Have you mentioned your name downstairs at the reception? No! Does anyone here know who you are? Again, no! Therefore you're not going to go out of your way to get mixed up in this affair! We're going to leave the hotel, and no one will ever know who we were. Early tomorrow morning we'll be off. This gentleman, the driver, too, for whom Mortimer's role is equally…"

"Ha," she snarled. "And you honestly believe that I—?"

"Go on…"

"—that I shall travel with you and not say word? That I shan't immediately make a full statement and ensure that everything possible is done to catch Mortimer's murderer?"

"Mortimer?" he bellowed. "I couldn't care a toss about him, nor what happens to any of your lovers, never mind this man, who certainly isn't Mortimer's murderer!"

"He is!"

"No, and you're not going to make a fool of me or get an innocent person into trouble."

"He's not innocent! He's at least an accomplice!"

"No, he's not, but even if he were, I couldn't care less! I forbid you to compromise me! You better keep your mouth shut!"

"No, I won't!"

They continued bawling and quarrelling like this on and on. For the most part Sponer didn't understand what was going on; however, he saw that here was a chance for him. He doubted that Montemayor could succeed in gagging the woman for good, but this quarrel could certainly delay the investigation, at least till he could make his getaway. To where? Abroad. Anywhere.

Of course, were he to flee, there was the danger that they might catch him before he was across the border. He had mentioned his name to the two of them; true, they might not have registered it or might well have forgotten it, but they knew that he was a taxi driver. It would therefore be the easiest thing in the world to track him down. And that very moment his eyes lit on Mortimer's passport that was lying on the table, and the idea occurred to him that it would possibly be easier to make his getaway using that rather than his own. At the border it would probably be the name of the suspect rather than that of the victim that was on the wanted list. He'd be safe only on Mortimer's passport, at least until such time as the dead man's name was reported everywhere in the papers.

He flipped open the passport. One passport photo is usually much like another, never mind the bearer. Moreover, the passports might very well be inspected en bloc, that is, collected up on the train, the names noted down, but the photos not checked for likeness with the bearers. And if it came to it, he could always try to swap his and Mortimer's photo. Perhaps he could get away with it.

From the moment the idea with the passport occurred to him, his brain went into overdrive. He slipped the passport in his pocket, which the quarrelling pair didn't notice. He moved towards the door. However, Winifred immediately shouted out. And, strange to say, so did Montemayor.

"Where are you going?" he cried. "Hold on!"

Sponer was already at the door. Montemayor, who was holding Winifred, couldn't release his grip on her to stop him. Sponer rushed into the hallway, slammed the bedroom door behind him, grabbed his coat from the hook where the page boy had hung it, pulled the key from the main door, stepped into the hall while slamming the door behind him, turned the key in the lock twice and thrust it in his pocket. Only then, as he was running along the corridor and was putting his coat on, did he realize that it must have been part of Montemayor's plan that he, Sponer, should stay in the hotel till the next morning and then leave, but only if he took Mortimer's things with him. It was now, of course, too late for him to go back and get them. Nor did he expect the enraged woman to keep quiet for long. Everything was collapsing about his ears. There was nothing left for him but to flee. He rushed down the stairs past the porter, who was half asleep, and dashed out into the street. The illuminated clock on the Opera House showed nearly two.

# 8

To the left, in a side street between the Bristol and the Grand Hotel, there were still some taxis. A few drivers, a couple of whom Sponer knew, were standing on the corner. He edged past them, went quickly to the last car and pulled the door open. "Next!" someone called out. A driver rushed up. Sponer got in hastily. He didn't know the driver. He gave the address of his flat. The driver slammed the door shut, got in, pulled out of the rank and drove off.

He'd get a few things from his flat, money above all—he had some savings—and then make his way straight to one of the railway terminals, no matter which, but best to the Südbahnhof, from where he'd be able to get across the Yugoslav border, imagining for some reason that from there it'd be easiest of all to get to Slovenia or Croatia, and disappear; he pictured there to be vast mountain tracts and huge forests there, dotted with isolated villages that the authorities had difficulty in looking after. It was now two o'clock; he could be at the station by a quarter to three, or three at the latest, because he'd literally not need more than a couple of minutes at his flat to throw together a few necessities, and he'd get the taxi to wait for him. As a matter of fact, if he were then to drive on to the Südbahnhof, it'd be a good idea to change cabs on the way to throw them off the scent, because by morning, when the matter would already be common knowledge, the driver would more than likely make a beeline for the police. Yes, he'd driven a man and his luggage from the Bristol to Sponer's flat and then on to the Südbahnhof, and he'd immediately become suspicious, and so on and so forth. That it'd be all over the morning papers he had no doubt; however, it no longer concerned him, because he was certain he'd reach the border first, well before the papers that carried Mortimer's name. He had at least eighteen hours' start on Mortimer's passport. And yet he was pretty sure that, having left Mortimer's luggage behind and departed so conspicuously, Montemayor himself would have to yield to his wife and make a statement. Clearly there was no way in which the latter could force the woman to keep quiet. It therefore made no difference whether the luggage had been left behind or not. The police might that very minute be in the process of taking down evidence, or have even finished doing so almost as soon as he had left the hotel room. Had the Montemayors got his name right, or just nearly right, it was likely detectives were already heading for his flat, or would do so before he had time to reach it himself, because the police operate with lightning speed in such cases, knowing full well that you've got to strike the iron while it's hot.

He knocked on the glass partition. The driver turned half around. Sponer called out to him Marie Fiala's flat.

Surely he needn't tell her what had happened. He'd merely ask her to fetch him a few things and the money from his flat, as he'd got himself into an awkward situation upon which he needn't elaborate; just ask her to do him a favour that she couldn't possibly refuse. All he had to do was to make it sound sufficiently urgent.

After all, she loved him. The night before, she had even cried. She'd go, all right. Let's face it, he thought, she ran no risk at all, because even if they found her in his flat, she could easily say...

The taxi pulled up in front of her house. He got out quickly and reached in his pocket to pay. It was empty. He'd thrown all his silver on the table at the Bristol. He had also left Mortimer's wallet on the table, it was an unpardonable mistake, because with the money that it contained, and the cheques, he could have... All he'd taken was the passport. Dammit! He swore and searched through all his pockets, and he'd even handed in his afternoon's takings to Haintl.

"Wait here!" he shouted to the driver, rushed up to the front door and rang the bell. At this moment he recalled that Haintl, when totting up the takings, had changed some of the coins for a banknote. Where was it? He felt in his breast pocket and found it.

While the driver was giving him his change, the front door was opened by the sleepy housekeeper, half hidden behind the main door and still in her nightclothes. He thrust a coin in her hand, said, "The Fialas'!" and started running up the stairs. The staircase was in darkness. He struck a couple of matches, and when he reached the Fialas' flat he rang the bell, then once more a few moments later.

It was dark behind the glass door. He stood and waited. It stank on the staircase. He rang a third time, keeping his finger on the bell. At that moment a light came on in the flat; he heard footsteps, a key was turned in the lock and the door opened.

It was Marie's father, who had thrown a coat over his shoulders and looked at Sponer.

"I've got to see Marie," said Sponer, walking in.

"Now?" Fiala asked.

"Yes."

"What's happened?"

"I've got to see her."

"Is it important?"

"Of course! Please wake her, and tell her to come out straight away."

"You've woken us all up anyway!"

"What took you so long?"

"I didn't know who it was in the middle of the night."

"All right, all right, but get her to come out now!"

Fiala looked at him. "What is it you want see her about?"

"I can't tell you. Just send her out. I'm in a hurry. Please!"

Fiala hesitated for a moment, muttered something, then turned around quickly and shuffled in his slippers towards a small door, opened it and went in. As he was closing the door, Sponer saw him turn on the light. Then he said something, and after that Marie's voice was heard. He reappeared shortly. "She's coming," he said. "Wait here in the meantime." He opened the door to the sitting room, turned the light on and saw Sponer in. He was restless, but afraid to say anything. Sponer slumped into an armchair. Fiala stood still for a moment, but said nothing; finally, he went into an adjoining room and shut the door behind him. There was the sound of a woman's voice asking a question to which he was heard to reply.

He was a minor clerk. Apart from Marie, he had two more children, ten and eight years of age; Sponer heard one of them talking in his sleep. Marie had also had a sister named Hedwig, but she had died.

The air in the room was stuffy and it smelt of food. On the stairs it had smelt the same, just as in the flat he rented from the Oxenbauers, and in the flats and on the stairs of the friends he had, and the acquaintances he sometimes visited. The air was stuffy and it smelt of food. Here people lived and then married, and their children in turn were brought up in flats where the air was stuffy and it smelt of food and a few other indefinable substances. Such was their life.

Sponer's father had been a captain in an infantry regiment. In his flat it might not have been so stuffy, nor had it smelt of food as strongly, except perhaps of fish on Fridays, but Sponer no longer recollected any of it. His mother had died long ago, and he himself was only just over eight when his father died, too. All he knew was how strange it had felt when the captain had been laid out between six candles, in uniform with the neat rows of shining buttons, the draped flag and his folded hands in the white suede gloves. A lot of people had been coming and going—medals, uniforms, shakos, and at the internment it had started to rain. But after the thin blue smoke of the abrupt salvo discharged over the grave had wafted away, everything else wafted away too, once and for all, and the succession of flats in which the child then lived stank of food and the air was stuffy. True, as an officer's son in 1917 he was accepted into a cadet school—there the air was, of course, good and the food, bad; but a year later he was back in the flats where the air was stuffy and it stank of food, and that's how it remained. That's what life was like. That's what his life was like, but now that it was coming to an end, it was nevertheless mighty difficult to bid farewell to it.

When Marie entered, he emerged from his short reverie and looked at her helplessly. She wore a pair of rubber-soled shoes and had a dressing gown over her shoulders. Her hair was hastily combed back and shimmered in thousands of loose strands against the light. Her face was very white and the look in her eyes was tense and alarmed. She stopped in the doorway.

"What is it?" she asked.

He got up. "Listen," he said, "I've got to ask you a favour."

"Yes," she said without taking her eyes off him. "What sort of favour?"

141

"Come closer," he said. "I've got to keep my voice down."

She approached him slowly. He reached in his pocket, drew out a cigarette and looked for matches. "You've got to," he said, "get me something out of my flat." He lit the cigarette.

She didn't reply immediately.

"Now?" she asked finally.

"Yes."

"From your flat?"

"Yes. A suit and some underwear. Preferably the dark-grey one. You know yourself where the underwear is. And a pair of shoes from under the washstand. And the things from the top of the washstand itself, together with the shaving gear. Put it all in the smaller suitcase, which is on top of the wardrobe. Not the big one, the small one. And then you've got to get me the money, too. It's in an envelope in the far left-hand corner of the table drawer. Here's the key." He pulled out a small bunch. "This is the key to the drawer, this is the key to the main door, this is the one to the flat. The room isn't locked... But the wardrobe is. This is the key to it." And he pulled out a single key from his pocket.

She had turned even paler and her lips were trembling. "What," she asked, "have you done?"

"Nothing," he said. "I've done nothing."

"Why do you need the things?"

"Because," he said, "I'm going away."

"For long?"

He made a vague gesture. "I don't know," he said. "Are you going to get the things for me then?"

"Why can't you get them yourself?"

"I'd rather not go back to my flat."

"Why not?"

"Don't ask me," he said. "I can't tell you. Anyway, you don't have to go. I merely asked you. You're free to say no. Only, in that case, this is the last you'll see of me."

He threw the bunch of keys on the table.

"And if I," she stammered, "get you the things? Will I see you again?"

"Then," he said, "perhaps."

There was an uncomfortable silence.

"Won't you tell me," she asked finally, "what's happened? Not because… because I want to pry into your affairs. But because I'm so scared for you!"

He looked at her, drew her close, kissed her and remained silent. She pressed her face against his shoulder. A few seconds later she straightened herself up again.

"All right," she said, "I'll go." And she took the keys from the table.

"Thank you," he said.

"I'll just get dressed," she said quickly and disappeared. He followed her with his eyes. In the adjoining room he heard a bed creak; shortly afterwards Fiala came in again. He wanted to ask something, but kept quiet.

"Marie," Sponer said, "has agreed to do something for

me. It won't take her longer than half an hour. Then she'll be back."

"What about you?" Fiala asked.

"I'll stay here in the meantime."

"What," asked Fiala, "is it that she has agreed to do?"

"She's going to get me something."

"From where?"

"From some friends. I've forgotten something there and would rather not go back myself. It's a small favour she's doing me, that's all. Please don't let it worry you. Go back to sleep, I beg you; you've no need to keep me company."

"Won't you," Fiala asked finally, "tell me what's going on?"

"No. It's not very interesting either."

"I've never," Fiala said, "spoken to you about your relationship with Marie. And anyway, you've always been very good to her, at least as far as I know, and if you didn't have the money to get married, there was nothing for it. But why do you have to come in the middle of the night and demand something so extraordinary? You're not going to… you're not going to get the girl to…"

"Mr Fiala," Sponer cried, "I've told you already that it's only a question of a small favour. Nothing to get worked up about. I…"

He fell silent because just then Marie entered. She was dressed and was wearing a coat. "I'm going now," she said. Fiala shook his head and went back to his room.

Sponer saw Marie out. "It's possible," he whispered, "someone may ask you where I am. If so, tell them you don't know, you came to my place only because you expected to find me in. For Heaven's sake, don't say I'm here. Do you understand?"

She just nodded.

He kissed her hands. She opened the front door. Then she went out and didn't return.

Just after the driver Georg Haintl had taken over from Sponer, there was a phone call to the garage for a cab to 73 Kaiserstrasse.

Haintl, who, as we already know, was slightly tipsy, filled up and drove to Kaiserstrasse.

He had to wait a little in front of No. 73, but then a party of five people in evening dress came out of the front door and bade one another goodbye: three set off towards Mariahilfer Strasse; while a man, and a woman in an ermine cape, got into the car. The man said, "Hotel Ambassador".

The journey took just over ten minutes. The hotel entrance was still lit brightly. A bellboy ran out and opened the door. The passengers alighted. The man put his hand in his pocket in order to pay, but found he had insufficient small change and wanted to offer the driver a note, whereupon the woman said she had some silver, and she went up to the driver and opened her evening bag.

"What's that on your back?" her companion suddenly asked.

"Where?" the woman enquired.

"On your cape," the man said. "The back's all dirty."

"Dirty?" the woman exclaimed.

"Yes," the man said, and pulled off one of his gloves and bent forward. "And it's wet, too," he said. When he withdrew his hand, his fingers were stained with a ruddy, coagulated gunge.

"But that's awful!" the woman shouted. "How on earth did it happen? It must be from the car!"

"From the car?" Haintl shouted loudly, still flushed with wine. "Are you saying my car's dirty?"

"Of course!" the man shouted. "The whole cape's dirty!"

A second bellboy came up, and the man and the boys examined the cape and confirmed that it was dirty, the woman trying all the while to turn her head sufficiently to see for herself.

"It's quite obvious it came from where you were sitting," the man shouted. "That's where the dirt stains are!" He opened the car door again and shouted to Haintl, "Turn the light on!" Haintl switched on the rear compartment light, got out of his seat, opened the door and all five of them looked in the back.

"There you are!" the man shouted, and pulled back the upholstery of the backrest. "It's all wet and dirty! The whole car's soaking wet! I noticed it as we were driving along!"

"But it's raining!" Haintl shouted.

"Yes, water, not shit!" the man shouted. "And the inside of the car's absolutely filthy!"

"From your shoes!" Haintl retorted.

By now a porter had also arrived on the scene, asked what the matter was and looked at the woman's back; the woman took off her cape and screamed that it was ruined. They all continued fingering the cape and the upholstery until they had all got their fingers dirty, and even Haintl had to admit that everything was dirty.

"What sort of dog cart is this?" the man shouted. "Whom does it belong to? We demand compensation! What is this filth! Everything's covered in it!"

They all walked into the light of the hotel entrance and examined their fingers. "It's all red!" one of the boys said. "Yes, reddish brown," the porter added; and the woman, who was still clutching her cape and trying to scrape the dirt off, suddenly clicked her fingers and exclaimed, "Ugh! Looks just like blood."

All at once they all fell silent. The man, wishing to lend support to his wife, said it really did look like blood, whereupon the bellboys turned pale, and the porter, now that the others agreed it was blood, added his voice, too, "Yes, yes, it's definitely blood." Haintl was absolutely horrified.

"How could it be?" the man shouted.

"I honestly don't know," Haintl stuttered, adding that he certainly wasn't responsible and so on. By now the manager had appeared, and a couple of passers-by had stopped and were staring. Haintl stammered that he himself had just taken over the car a quarter of an hour ago, and that the blood must already have been there.

"Who had the car before you?" the manager asked.

"Another driver," stammered Haintl, and thought of Sponer.

"Who?" the man shouted, and Haintl mentioned Sponer's name.

In the end, Haintl had to go to the police station. The man and the woman also drove the short distance in another car; and so it was that Jack Mortimer's blood, which Sponer had only partially succeeded in washing off in the dark, had come to be in Bräunerstrasse for the second time.


There it was established that the blood was not, as the porter at the Ambassador had first imagined, from a quarried deer, a goose or chicken whose throat had been slit and which someone had been transporting in the taxi, but the blood of someone shot just a few hours previously; they also found the two bullets that had gone through Mortimer's body and penetrated the car's bodywork; and Haintl, having been told to leave the car at the police station, was driven, accompanied by two detectives, first to the Brandeis garage and, since the only person there was the car washer, on to Sponer's flat. In the meantime the Brandeis family were alarmed, but of course knew nothing. One of the detectives rang the front doorbell; the door was opened and, accompanied by the startled porter, they mounted the stairs, woke up the Oxenbauers, and entered Sponer's room. What with the examination of the blood-stained interior of the car at the police station and everything else, it was, by then, gone two in the morning.

Of course, they hardly expected to find Sponer in his room, though it was possible he could still turn up. The manner in which he had handed the car over to Haintl gave the impression he thought he had got rid of all traces of blood. He was evidently convinced he had. After a short session with Oxenbauer and his daughter, neither of whom had anything material to say because they had both gone to bed at about half past ten and were therefore not aware of Sponer having returned to his flat twice, they were released, but told to keep to their rooms, as was the porter, though the couple did not go back to bed, but started discussing the night's unprecedented events. In the meantime the detectives continued interrogating Haintl and began a thorough search of Sponer's room. They noted the two French newspapers, and also broke into the wardrobe and found the wet suit.

Having got that far, however, no one had as yet thought of the table drawer (the table was covered over with a blanket), when Marie Fiala appeared. She had found the front door downstairs, which had an old-fashioned lock, closed, of course, but not locked, which the porter in his confusion and panic had forgotten to do. Her heart began to beat.

Although it was dark, being on familiar territory, she rushed up the stairs confidently. The door to the flat was not fully locked, and she entered by turning the key slightly. By now she was almost convinced something was the matter, though she didn't know what, for Sponer had said virtually nothing to her. The detectives and Haintl, as well as the Oxenbauers and the porter in the other rooms, heard the sound of the key being turned in the lock. The light was immediately switched off in Sponer's room, and those waiting in the other rooms fell silent. Marie entered and noticed the strip of light showing under the door of the Oxenbauers' room. For a moment she hesitated. If it had been just up to her, she'd have immediately left the place, rushed back to Sponer, and said this, that and the other had happened. The fact that she saw a strip of light under the door could, of course, have an innocent explanation. However, why couldn't she hear anyone talking or moving about? She stood stock-still for a full two or three minutes, and listened.

But all she heard was her own heart pounding, like it had pounded the whole way there, like it had pounded when Sponer had turned up, like it had pounded all those long years when she had heard nothing else. And she followed that heart of hers, and Sponer's urgent request to fetch his things, and entered the room.

She had hardly stepped over the threshold, when she was grabbed and held fast. She let out a cry. At the same time someone turned the light on. She saw the two detectives and Haintl, and the next moment the Oxenbauers and the porter also rushed in.

They were evidently expecting Sponer himself, because Haintl cried out the moment the light was switched on that it was only Marie.

"Who?" asked one of the detectives, a dark-haired, stocky man.

"Marie Fiala," Haintl said. "Sponer's girlfriend."

"Yes, that's right, his girlfriend," the Oxenbauer girl added immediately.

But Haintl turned to Marie and shouted, "For God's sake, how could he have done such a thing!"

"Done what?" Marie asked, as white as a sheet.

The other detective, a tall, blond, slightly thick-set man, immediately motioned to Haintl to keep quiet.

"What has he done?" Marie repeated.

"What are you looking for here?" the blond detective asked.

"What has he done?" Marie screamed.

Haintl shrugged his shoulders.

"I want to know what brought you here!" the detective shouted. "Do you hear me?"

"Yes," she stammered.

"So, what are you looking for here?"

"I'm looking for…" she stuttered. "I wanted…"

"What did you want?"

"I wanted to see… Ferdinand," she finally said.

"Now?"

"Yes."

"And where have you been up to now?" the other detective enquired.

At the precise moment she didn't know what to say, for she was still completely confused; the only thing she knew was that she mustn't betray Sponer. She mustn't tell them that she'd come from her house and that Sponer was still there. It was obvious something dreadful must have happened, but she had not a moment's hesitation in her resolve not to betray him.

"Now, are you going to tell us?" the detective shouted.

She finally said she'd been at her friend's place where they'd been darning sheets.

"All this time?"

"Yes."

"And where did you get the key from?" the blond detective asked.

"Which key?"

"The front-door key!"

"The front door," she said, "was already open."

They all looked at the housekeeper.

"What?" the housekeeper stammered. "Open? That means I must have…"

"And the key to the flat?" the stocky detective asked.

"The key to the flat?"

"Yes, the key to the flat!"

"The door to the flat, too, was open."

"But you still can't open it without a key," the stocky man said.

She no longer knew what to say. The detective in the meantime put his hand into her coat pocket and brought out the key. "So, where did you get it?"

She was silent.

"Where did you get it?" the man repeated.

She clenched her teeth.

"You don't want to say?"

"No."

"It's hardly necessary," the blond detective said. "It's obvious you must have got it from Sponer. Where did he give it to you? Where is he?"

She remained silent.

"If you won't answer," the blond detective said, "I'll do it for you. You must have got the key just a short time ago, otherwise you'd have come earlier. And where were you till now? Darning sheets? A likely story! You were at home. Sponer could have given you the key only when you were at home. He stayed at your place and sent you here with the key. Obviously he wants you to get something for him. Isn't that so?"

"Yes," she said. She realized that she had made a terrible mistake in not answering the questions. Her silence had revealed more than answers would have done, for it enabled the others to draw the obvious conclusion. Now that they'd caught her out, they'd also search her flat. They'd do it in any case, because she was Sponer's girlfriend. Unless she managed to distract the detectives, they would find Sponer.

"And what was it that he wanted you to bring him?" the blond detective asked.

"Money," she answered. "But for Heaven's sake, tell me what he has…"

"What does he need money for? Is he planning to escape?"

"I don't know," she said. "He just wanted it. But if you don't want to tell me…"

"Where is the money?" the other one asked.

They didn't disclose what had happened. She looked at Haintl, but he only shrugged his shoulders.

"Where is the money?" the stocky one repeated.

"In the drawer," she said after a moment's pause. The blond one removed the cover from the desk, but couldn't pull the drawer out.

"You've got the key," she suddenly added, "It's with the other ones."

The stocky detective gave the blond one the key.

"It's on the left at the back," she said.

They took out the envelope.

"Is this it?" the stocky one asked.

"Yes."

They looked inside. All the others also stared with curiosity. The envelope contained just a few notes. "Is that all?" the stocky one asked.

"Yes," she said.

They had evidently expected to find more, obviously all the money that Sponer had taken from the murdered person, whoever he was. If it hadn't been for the fact that they also wanted to investigate the robbery, they wouldn't have remained there a moment longer, but would have left immediately to apprehend Sponer. Now, however, they were disappointed to find only Sponer's meagre savings. The stocky one threw the envelope on the table.

"And where," he asked, "is the rest of the money?"

It had not yet dawned on the two detectives why it was that Marie was suddenly so willing to answer their questions. Now that the main object of her mission was lying there on the table, she could take it to Sponer.

Quick as a flash she grabbed the money, made a dash for the door, ran out and slammed the door of the flat. Before the amazed company had realized what was happening, she had slammed the door behind her and was standing in the dark; then she ran not down the stairs, but up without a moment's hesitation. A woman almost always does the right thing instinctively.

She was already on the landing and round the bend before the others stormed out of the flat. They naturally all ran down the stairs, continually stumbling, cursing and striking matches. The detectives were more astute, however; instead of running, they slid down the banister. They were also the first to reach the front door, which they tore open, and ran out into the street. A few moments later the others were also at the bottom of the stairs and likewise ran out into the street.

# 9

A S SOON AS THE COAST WAS CLEAR, Marie also ran down. The front door was open; she carefully peered out into the street and saw that it was deserted. However, at the very moment when she stepped out of the house, one of the detectives—the tall one—and Haintl, were already on their way back. Finding the neighbouring streets deserted, they had no doubt surmised that Marie was probably still in the house. That it hadn't occurred to them why they hadn't heard her running down the stairs when they were following her could probably be best explained by the fact that they themselves were making so much noise in the pursuit.

As soon as they turned the corner, the two of them immediately saw Marie and broke into a run. She started in the other direction, towards Mariahilfer Strasse. At that very moment the Oxenbauers, the housekeeper and the second detective came round the corner ahead of her. The first lot shouted to the second to stop Marie. She therefore ran as quickly as she could diagonally across the street, ducking and weaving to evade the first two, and ran on with all six of them in hot pursuit.

She didn't run towards her house, but in the opposite

direction. She thought that in this way she'd be able to prevent them finding Sponer, for as long as she managed to keep running, the detectives would be much too preoccupied with catching her to bother about Sponer.

The detectives and Haintl ran in front, while the Oxenbauers and the housekeeper brought up the rear. Everyone, including those who in actual fact were not at all involved in the matter, seemed hell-bent on not letting Marie and Sponer get away with it. All through the chase the detectives would issue shrill whistling sounds.

Marie, of course, immediately realized that very soon she'd be out of breath and wouldn't be able to maintain the pace, and that they'd catch up with her even if she ran like mad. Also, a policeman on the beat, attracted by the detectives' whistles, dived out in front of her.

The pursuers shouted to him to stop Marie, but he failed to grasp their meaning simply because she threw herself straight in his arms and gasped, "They're chasing me!" Thereupon she staggered behind him and stood there panting for a second.

"Stop!" the policeman shouted at the officials who, being in plain clothes, he failed to identify as fellow guardians of the law, bearing down upon him at full pelt. They, of course, took no notice of his command. "Stop!" he shouted once more, and as they were by now very close and were clearly intent on grabbing hold of Marie, without any hesitation he socked them over the head with his rubber truncheon.

One of them went down instantly, while the other began to reel; Haintl, too, ran up now, helped one of the injured detectives to his feet, and while confusion reigned and the ill-treated detective took pains to explain to the policeman that he was an idiot, Marie was once more able to continue her getaway.

Now, however, the pursuers were no longer able to keep up the pace and, in addition, Haintl had his work cut out helping the seriously hurt detective to stay in the chase. The Oxenbauers were far behind by now, and when Marie reached the corner of the street and looked round, she could no longer see any of them.

In two or three minutes she came to Mariahilfer Strasse, the section that runs from Westbahnhof to Schönbrunn Palace. She ran directly towards the city centre, but after a few steps realized this was a mistake. It would have been better to have run in the opposite direction, since there among the houses and in the dim side streets she stood more of a chance to shake them off her track. However, it was too late to turn back. Moreover, some of the passers-by who were still about even at that late hour would notice the chase, for the pursuers were shouting and whistling, though Marie still had such a good lead over them that she would always be somewhat ahead of them before the passers-by took any notice. She finally decided to jump into a taxi and headed for a line of three or four waiting cabs, but then ran past the astonished drivers after she realized she couldn't in the time available tell any of the drivers to drive off just like that, immediately; and besides, the engine might well not start straight away, or the driver himself would have noticed the pursuers in the meantime and simply refused to drive off. After she had run past the taxis, however, it struck her that she no longer heard the whistling and shouting of her pursuers; she stopped, gasping for breath, and saw that they had commandeered one of the taxis in order to drive after her.

For a moment she thought that her luck had run out. Then she staggered towards an approaching tram.

It was, of course, not a regular tram at this time of night, but a service vehicle with a high superstructure, used nightly to inspect and maintain the overhead electric cables. A second car, a type of trailer carrying the necessary equipment, was coupled to the first. The two tramcars were travelling quite fast. The headlights dazzled her; she tried to grab hold of the first car and jump on board, but was plunged into darkness after the lights had passed, and she missed her chance. The second tramcar then followed, but she soon saw there was no way she could jump on; only when the rear end of the car came up level did she see a pair of handles, or rather a type of iron clamps forming some steps. She grabbed hold of one of them and, due to the speed of the car, was immediately thrown off balance since, in her confused and exhausted state, she had not thought of running in the same direction as the car after she had grabbed hold of the step.

Nevertheless, being dragged along, holding on for dear life, she managed to reach the handle with her second hand and pull herself up, whereupon she then felt herself being carried along. What's more, she finally managed to find a foothold. For a second or two she just hung on, completely exhausted.

In the meantime the motorcar was in hard pursuit and catching up. They had seen Marie's manoeuvre and were calling to the driver of the tram to stop. However, this tram wasn't stopping anywhere, except for maintenance, and moreover the driver had no idea what was going on, perhaps he didn't even hear anything. In any case, he just let them carry on shouting and drove on.

Marie in the meantime had clambered up the iron steps and tumbled over the railing into the trailer. There was no one there, for the crew were all in the front car. For a few seconds she lay panting on the floor, then she stood up and looked over the top of the railing.

The car with her pursuers was closing the gap fast, but at this point the tram turned left into the ring road. Before the tram turned, the pursuers had tried to come up level, they had opened the car door, and the blond detective was standing on the running board, ready to jump onto the trailer. The car was already alongside when the tram veered left. The gap between the tram rails and the boarding step narrowed so quickly that the car was forced to brake suddenly. It was too late, however. The off-side front wheel caught the edge of the boarding step and was jerked sideways; the car went out of control, and the detective on the running board was thrown onto the road.

He lay there, apparently injured. The others ignored him, however, jumped out of the car, and ran after the tram.

The tram gathered speed along the ring road. Haintl and the remaining detective, realizing they could no longer keep up, screamed and bellowed at the top of their voices. Meanwhile, in the front tramcar they were by now aware of what had happened, but the driver, because he either still hadn't noticed anything, or else had a guilty conscience, as maybe he thought he was responsible for the accident, drove on regardless. The others, however, drew his attention to the pursuers. There was a brief exchange of words, the tram finally came to a halt, and Marie, who had still not been noticed by the people in the front tramcar, jumped down from the trailer.

In front of her was a narrow side road flanked by trees and some bushes. She ran into the cover it afforded. In the meantime the detective and Haintl came running up, completely out of breath. They must have noticed Marie leap from the trailer, and without bothering to explain anything to the people on the tram also dashed into the cover of the side road.

On the far side stood a large sprawling building, still brightly lit. Between the side road and the building was a lane on either side of which there was a long line of parked taxis and private cars.

The building was a suburban hotel, the ground floor accommodating a coffee house and a large, popular entertainment complex.

Marie ran across the road and along the line of parked cabs. However, as she approached the entrance to the complex, she became increasingly conspicuous on account of all the bright lights, and on the spur of the moment she jumped into one of the cabs.

Its driver, like the majority of the drivers, was not standing by his cab. However, Marie's pursuers hadn't overlooked the possibility that she might jump into one of the cabs and drive off, and they wanted to forestall her manoeuvre. What they evidently didn't know was which car she had got into. So they began to search the nearest cars by opening the doors and looking inside. They could no longer summon the strength to shout and draw attention, for they were completely out of breath.

They simply opened and closed the cab doors, with the result that one of the drivers approached them and asked them where they wanted to go. Needless to say, they didn't reply.

In the meantime Marie tried to make herself inconspicuous in the back of the cab she had jumped into. She couldn't ask the driver to take her anywhere for the simple reason that there was no driver about. However, presently the driver appeared with a group of people who were prepared to get into the taxi and gave him an address.

Five people were about to get in and soon noticed there was already someone crouching in the back. Normally one would, of course, have assumed that the taxi had already been taken, but Marie remained silent for so long, cowering in a corner, that it was not until someone had sat on her lap—the driver had switched on the light in the back only a couple of seconds after he had got into his seat—that it suddenly dawned on those getting into the taxi that something was not in order, and they immediately asked what the person was doing in the back. There was therefore nothing left for Marie but to jump out of the taxi onto the road, skirt round the vehicle and dash through the gates of the entertainment complex.

Her pursuers, who were by now quite close as they went through the cars, saw what she'd done and ran after her.

It must have been a private function, or rather the tail end of one—this was no longer the season for public ones. In the cloakroom, as Marie dashed through, people were already in the process of collecting their overcoats. Tickets at the entrance to the reception rooms were no longer being checked with the result that she was able to enter unchallenged. Here there was still a fairly large crowd of people among whom she could disappear. She tore off her coat and dived into the crowd. There were hundreds of women there, all looking much like one another and, indeed, no better dressed than she was.

Having burst into the hotel, it was while Haintl and the

detective began accosting all the womenfolk in search of Marie, which naturally created the impression that both of them were drunk, and the staff were about to apprehend and eject them, that Marie managed to dash across the floor of the next reception room and reach the passageway between the private rooms and the coffee house, for she was familiar with the general layout, having already been there two or three times previously with Sponer. She hurried through the coffee house, back into the street and, half-running, half-walking, and set off in the direction of her house. She unlocked the front door, rushed up the stairs and entered her flat, completely exhausted.

However, Sponer was no longer there.

He had waited in the living room, nervously smoking and staring vacantly before him, and at first had thought for a few moments about Marie, but then his thoughts drifted to Mortimer and Mortimer's murderer, and to the underworld from which they had both emerged and to which they had both returned—one living, the other dead.

Since the beginning of the world there was the upper world and the nether world—the underworld. Not just one, but two worlds—that then was the world. Since the beginning of mankind there were the *obermenschen* and the *untermenschen*, not just one mankind as such, but two—that then was mankind. As a consequence there were the high and the low, the noble and the ignoble, the saints and the sinners, the gods and the demons—that was mankind. But also, since the beginning of mankind it was not a question of noble or ignoble, upper or lower, evil or good; but rather noble, ignoble, upper, lower, evil and good, all rolled into one—that then was man.

Since time immemorial there were gods and demons, virtue and vice, saints and sinners, angels and beasts, lords and knaves. Oft were the lords the knaves, and the knaves the lords. Never were the lords and the knaves one and the same. But each had a touch of the lord and a touch of the knave in him, a touch of the reigning and a touch of the slaving, the conscientious and the ruthless, the animal and the spiritual, the loving and the hating, the shining and the darkening in him.

The underworld had again and again broken through the Earth's ridiculously thin crust, and since time immemorial the demon would rear up in men's hearts.

One believed it was possible to drive crime under the asphalt and the concrete of cities, under multi-storey buildings, roadways and churches. It could be confined, so it was thought, in canals, under bridges, in abandoned cellars... But that was not true at all. It rose, it penetrated into houses, stations, offices. It penetrated into Mortimer's bank, settled at his writing desk; it travelled with him to Europe, followed him invisibly, like Satan followed Judas Iscariot, and dragged him down again into the underworld, without a sound, without a trace, without leaving a single clue. He had sat there dead, as dead as a doornail, in the taxi, with three bullet holes in him—that was all. No sound, no shadow, no sign of the murderer; the dead man had just sat there as though not dead at all, his eyes fixed in a sidelong indifferent stare, and it was only when Sponer shook him that he slumped forward and lay between the suitcase and the seat, and Sponer then realized that the man was in cahoots with the Devil, and that Mortimer was now trying to drag him, too, down into hell. How was he allowed to do so, who gave him the right, why had the guilty one gone free, why hadn't Mortimer clung to the real murderer?…

Sponer looked up with a start. Fiala had entered from the adjoining room.

"Marie isn't back yet?" he asked.

"No," said Sponer, and he looked at him blankly.

"It's already a quarter past three," Fiala said.

"A quarter past three?"

"Where on earth have you sent her?"

"Who? Marie?"

"Yes. She's been gone more than half an hour."

It wouldn't have taken her more than a few minutes to reach Sponer's place, then another ten minutes at most to collect his things—for she knew, of course, where they were—and then another couple of minutes to return home. He had told her to come back, that it was urgent; she herself must, of course, have realized that. Why then wasn't she back yet? Perhaps, he thought, perhaps...

"Well?" Fiala asked.

"What?" Sponer shouted nervously.

"Where is Marie?"

"I don't know!" Sponer replied. "I'm waiting for her myself!"

Something must have happened, otherwise she'd have returned by now. Obviously the Montemayors had already called the police, and it was lucky for him that he hadn't gone to his flat. If, however, they'd arrested Marie, he'd never be able to get his things, above all the money. How then would he escape? And besides, they'd ask Marie where he was, and although, of course, he had asked her not to say anything and she'd keep her mouth shut, nevertheless they would in any case come and search her flat, for it was likely that...

He jumped to his feet. "What's the exact time?" he asked Fiala.

"Almost half past," Fiala said. "Tell me, where's Marie?"

"I'll go and meet her," Sponer said. "She must almost be here by now. I'll ask her to come straight up."

With that he dashed out of the room. Fiala watched him go. Sponer opened the door to the apartment, which was not locked, closed it behind him, listened for a moment in the darkness of the landing, and ran down the stairs. The front door was locked. He struck a match, looked for the housekeeper's door and knocked. After a couple of seemingly

167

endless minutes the housekeeper finally appeared, woken for the second time.

"Open the door!" Sponer commanded.

"Why didn't you get the key from the Fialas?" she asked.

"Come on!" Sponer shouted. "Open the door!"

She shuffled to the door, mumbling to herself, and unlocked it. He quickly peered into the street and then stepped out. She closed the door behind him.

He first hurried in the direction from which Marie would have to come—if indeed she came. However, if she did, then she probably wouldn't be alone. He therefore turned back, went past her front door, and stopped round the next corner.

The street was completely silent except for the flapping of a loose strip of lead under a roof guttering in the damp wind. After some time two people appeared from a side street, crossed the road, and disappeared at the far end.

He waited a further quarter of an hour. Nobody came. He was now convinced they'd caught Marie. And soon people would come, burst into Fiala's house, and search the apartment.

He could not escape without money. At best he could try to lie low somewhere in the city, but there was no one left at whose place he could shelter. Besides, wherever he went, they'd immediately report him. So, from now on, all he could do was stay on the move and hope they wouldn't find him. However, after a couple of days they'd be sure to catch him.

He might just as well give himself up now. It was as short as it was long. He really didn't have a choice.

He was now no longer Jack Mortimer; he was no longer even Sponer, the driver; he was no longer anybody.

He was finished. However, when he realized that the game was up, he didn't do what he would have done if he were still Sponer, namely go and report to the police. He did what Jack Mortimer would probably have done in his shoes. He glanced once more along the silent streets and then walked on.

He went to Marisabelle's.

The street lights flickered and swayed. His steps echoed between the bleak, grimy fronts of the suburban houses. However, as he drew near the city centre, he became aware of a continuous clanging and rattling sound, and the clip-clop of horses' hooves, as if an occupying force were approaching while the city slept: it was the traffic from the country, coming to supply the early morning markets. When he turned into Burggasse, it was full of vans and carts. A straggling mass of draught horses and vehicles, with small lamps on the shafts of horse-drawn carts or dangling above the coachmen's seats, were all bathed in the dim light of gas-lit street lanterns. Brass-inlaid leather finery dangled from the horses' halters; their drivers, huddled in coats and blankets, crouched half asleep; milk carts laden with metal churns rattled over the cobbles; and the smell of horses and petrol, mixed with the smell of fruit, vegetables and autumn flowers, hung in the air.

Every night, out on the farms, carts are loaded, horses are brought out of the grange stables; every night a train of these conveyances performs its ghostly journey, which goes on for several hours at walking speed. Isolated farmsteads swim into view along the sides of the road and then sink back into the darkness; a wind blows from the wet fields. These are replaced by the brick walls of the suburbs; the roads are now paved; heavy hooves strike the surface noisily; the carts sway from side to side; the city finds its reflection in the horses' huge eyes as in a dream; and as in a dream the people perceive the rattle of the carts outside their bedroom windows. Come the morning, everything's gone. The horses, as they are unharnessed from the empty carts on their farms where snowflakes or blossoms fall from the fruit trees, have forgotten that it was a city they'd been to at night, and the city has forgotten that a procession of carts comes and goes every night.

Sponer hurried down Burggasse alongside the rumbling and clanking carts, then turned right onto Lastenstrasse, which was equally busy. Only at Karlsplatz did he turn off, and the clatter and rattle died away in the distance.

It must have been close on four in the morning when he reached Marisabelle's house.

He went up to the front gate and rang the bell. While he was waiting, he suddenly fancied he could see Marisabelle's outline in the shadow of the gate, like the other morning when her shadow receded as she shrank back, and the gate closed. He had not followed her then. Now, however, he would go through the gate, and the fact that she had backed away wouldn't help her in the slightest. He would reach her.

Finally a light appeared in the glass panes over the gate; he could hear the sound of approaching steps echoing in the entrance hall, and the gate opened. A porter—a man of about fifty-five or sixty, clean-shaven and casually dressed—peered out of the gate and asked Sponer what he wanted.

"I must speak to Fräulein von Raschitz," Sponer said.

"Who?" the porter asked.

"Fräulein von Raschitz."

"What, now?"

"Yes."

"That's not possible," the porter replied.

"Why not?" Sponer asked.

"What's it about?"

"It's urgent."

"What do you mean, urgent? Can't it wait till the morning?"

"No," Sponer said. "It can't."

"Can't you leave a message?" the porter enquired.

"A message?" Sponer asked. "No, I can't leave a message."

"But I can't let you in all the same. You'll wake up the whole house if you…"

"If I what?"

"If you ring."

"Possibly," Sponer said. "However, I have to speak to the lady."

"Is it so urgent?"

"Yes."

"Can't you speak to the major?"

"No," Sponer said and stepped through the gate. He knew that he would speak to Marisabelle. Now that he was so close to her on such a night, a porter was no longer an obstacle. The servants, too, wouldn't prevent him, nor the major, not even Marisabelle's mother. He pushed the porter aside and entered. The man immediately grabbed his arm.

Sponer tore himself free. "Keep away!" Sponer yelled out and pushed past him into the entrance. It was similar to the one in Prinz-Eugen-Strasse, where he had approached Marisabelle the first time. He could see the staircase on the left. A large electric ceiling lantern cast everything into light and shade. "Which one's her flat?" he asked as he headed for the staircase.

The porter ran after him and asked if he was out of his mind or what.

"I have to speak to the lady," Sponer barked. "Do you understand?"

"But you can't wake them up at this hour!"

"That's for me to decide!" Sponer retorted. "Which one's their flat?"

The porter stood there, not knowing what to do.

"Well?" Sponer shouted.

"First floor, the one on the left," the man said finally.

Sponer immediately made for the staircase, followed a moment later by the porter. He turned the landing light on and walked up the stairs, while the porter remained below, looking up at him.

On the first floor Sponer read: Raschitz.

He rang the bell.

While he waited for the door to open, he rested his hand on the heavy, polished door, then leant forward and let his forehead, too, rest against the door.

He had closed his eyes.

There was no smell of cooking or stale air on these stairs. The people who lived here didn't have to drive a taxi for a living and wouldn't be suspected of having killed Jack Mortimer. Although the difference was just a single rank, Major von Raschitz lived here, and not the son of Captain Sponer. Also, Marisabelle lived here, not Marie. One was an aristocrat, the other a simple seamstress now under arrest because of him; one had sacrificed everything for him, the other hadn't even condescended to listen to him. However, he knew that she would listen to him now. One listens to a person who comes in the scarlet cloak of a murderer, even if he is only a driver.

He could hear steps approaching. He straightened up. A housemaid with a dressing gown over her shoulders opened the door.

173

"What's the matter?" she asked softly. "What do you want?"

"I want to speak to Fräulein Marisabelle."

"To Fräulein Marisabelle? Now? You must be mad!"

"Listen," he said, "I must speak to her. It's very important. I wouldn't have come otherwise."

"But I can't wake her up now."

"You must!"

She stood there, indecisive. She was still very young and rather pretty.

They looked at each other, and when she saw his eyes maybe she somehow realized that something special and important might have occurred between a man with such beautiful eyes and Marisabelle, which explained the urgency of the matter at this time of night.

"What's your name then?" she finally asked.

"Sponer," he said. "However, there's no need to mention my name to the lady. Just say someone needs to speak to her urgently."

"Keep your voice down," she whispered. "You'll wake the house up if you haven't already done so!"

"Go and tell her," he pleaded.

She fell silent and looked at him again, and he looked at her too.

"All right," she finally whispered. "I'll tell the lady."

Then she closed the door and he heard her scurry off.

Sponer stood there, and after a few moments he heard the porter take a couple of steps down below on the staircase, obviously wanting to know whether Sponer was still there. Then it became quiet again, the porter was probably listening to what was going on above. The maid opened the door again.

"She's not in," she whispered.

"Who's not in?" Sponer stammered.

"The lady."

"What do you mean?"

"She's not at home."

"How come she's not home?"

"She was invited out last night and she's not back yet."

"At this hour?"

"Yes."

"It's not true!" Sponer shouted dejectedly.

She furrowed her eyebrows.

"What's not true?" she asked.

"That she's not in! You simply don't want to announce me."

"So," she said, "you don't believe me. Of course, I can't ask you to see for yourself. Whether or not you believe me is up to you."

With that she closed the door. Sponer tried to put his foot in the way, but was too late. He knocked loudly on the door and shouted that he believed what she'd just told him, but he at least wanted to know when Marisabelle would return. There was no answer. He stood there fuming, and finally descended the stairs.

The porter was standing down below.

"Well?" he asked.

"They said she's not in," Sponer muttered.

"There, you see!" the porter said, and switched off the light on the staircase.

"What do you mean, 'You see'?" Sponer shouted. "You yourself thought she was in! Where else would she be! Of course she's upstairs!"

"She was invited out," the porter said. "I saw her leave the house some time before ten o'clock. If she's not back yet, she'll…"

Sponer had motioned to him to stop talking.

They stood there together in the entrance, and heard the sound of a car drive up to the house; people got out, conversed in front of the house, and then bade one another goodbye. Sponer recognized Marisabelle's voice.

A key was inserted into the lock at the top of the front gate, but was not turned since the gate was, of course, unlocked; nevertheless, the porter's keys on the inside fell to the floor, and the gate opened.

Marisabelle and her brother entered.

She was wearing an evening dress and a fur; he was wearing a coat over a tuxedo and a black top hat.

While the porter greeted them and picked up his keys from the floor, and the young Raschitz asked him what the matter was, Marisabelle took a couple of steps and recognized Sponer.

*

She stopped dead in her tracks, and the young Raschitz looked up.

Sponer went up to Marisabelle.

She didn't flinch, however; she merely stared at him, perfectly composed, for she probably sensed from the circumstances and the expression on his face that something quite extraordinary must have happened. He stood there in front of her, bowed, and whispered something in her ear.

At that moment the young Raschitz approached and asked her in a shrill and demanding voice what this man wanted.

Marisabelle, without looking at him, motioned him away with a movement of her head, while Sponer ignored him completely and continued speaking to her imploringly.

Marisabelle blushed.

"What on earth's the chap going on about?" the young man shouted. "Shall I get rid of him?"

Marisabelle, as white as a sheet, turned to face him.

"Go away," she said in a peculiarly forced voice. "I have to talk to him."

"What does he want from you?"

"I can't tell you. Go away!"

"Why should I?"

"You can see he wants to tell me something."

"What did he say to you?"

"It's none of your business."

"I won't tolerate him annoying you like this!"

"Leave me alone!" she shouted, her words as sharp as tacks. "You've no right to boss me about!"

He looked at her, nonplussed.

"Leave me alone!" she repeated. "I've got to talk to him, don't you understand?"

He looked at her completely flabbergasted, then raised his hands in the white doeskin gloves as if about to strike someone.

"Clear off!"

He dropped his hands, stood there for a moment, then turned, cursing, and strode furiously towards the staircase. They heard him walk up the stairs.

The porter stared at them. Marisabelle motioned to him to leave. He hastily locked the gate and withdrew into his flat.

Marisabelle looked at Sponer; her eyes were wide open and her lips were trembling.

"It's not possible," she finally said. "I must have misunderstood what you said."

He shrugged his shoulders.

"You understood me quite correctly," he said.

"Who's the dead person then?" she stammered.

"An American," he said. "His name is Jack Mortimer, a gangster, someone shot him. However, it's irrelevant who he is and who the murderer was. The fact is, I can no longer prove it wasn't me who killed him. There's nothing more I can do to convince anyone I'm not guilty. They're already looking for me. I don't believe for one moment they'll think

I'm here, but nevertheless it could be dangerous for you that I'm here…"

She made a dismissive gesture.

"The fact is, I'm done for," he said. "By tomorrow they'll arrest me. All I needed to do was to go to the police and report I had a dead person in the car and didn't know who'd shot him, and in the end they'd have had to believe me and I'd have been released. Instead, I've done just the opposite, and have landed myself in no end of a mess. I can see it all now. If I hadn't done it, I wouldn't be here now. If I didn't have blood on my hands, which I hadn't spilt, I wouldn't have seen you again. If I hadn't been in a mess, I wouldn't have been able to come here and tell you I love you."

Then he fell on his knees, threw his arms around her, and buried his face in her lap.

Instead of extricating herself and pushing him away, she leant back and closed her eyes; her hands groped for a moment in the darkness and then strayed over his hair and his shoulders. He was overcome by a convulsive movement like that of a man sobbing.

"Come now, get up," she finally whispered. "We can't stay here. Come with me!"

He stood up, feeling slightly giddy. She took him by the hand and led him up the stairs. They stopped in front of her flat.

"Wait here a moment," she said.

She took a key out of her handbag and opened the door. After a few moments she reappeared. She had a bunch of keys in her hand.

"Follow me," she said. They ran up the next flight of stairs and, taking one of the keys from the bunch, she opened the door to an apartment. On the brass plate he read: "Dorfmeister".

They stepped into an entrance hall. She switched the light on, locked the door and left the key in the lock. She opened the next door, they entered a room that appeared to have been unoccupied for a long time, then they went into a second room, a bedroom, in which the furniture was covered with sheets and the curtains had been taken down. The chandelier, too, was covered by a large, shroudlike sheet, through which the bulbs shone dimly after Marisabelle had pulled the switch. The air was stale and smelt of camphor.

"Where are we?"

"Some relatives of ours live here," she said. "But they're not here now. They're away at the moment."

They stood in the doorway and looked into the room, which was in semi-darkness and appeared extraordinarily large and bare. He felt for her hands and began to squeeze them. He lifted up her hands and buried his face in them.

She leant against the wall and looked at him. She opened her mouth a couple of times as if to say something.

"Why," she finally asked, "did you do it?"

He pretended not to hear and smothered the palms of her hands with kisses.

"Why did you do it?" she repeated.

He looked up.

"Do what?" he asked.

In the dim yellow light of the shrouded chandelier her face shimmered like pale, translucent alabaster illuminated from within, and her eyes, unnaturally large, stared out from under her long, glinting eyelashes.

"What?" he asked once more. "What have I done?" And he slowly lowered his face and kissed her on the mouth.

She did not return his kiss. She waited until he had withdrawn his lips from hers, and then said, "Why did you kill that man?"

He didn't understand at first what she said.

"What?" he asked.

"Why did you kill him?" she repeated.

"Me?" he asked. "Who?"

"Jack Mortimer."

"Jack Mortimer?"

"Yes."

"You believe I did it?"

"Yes."

He straightened up.

"Are you out of your mind?" he yelled.

"Why?" she asked, and contracted her eyebrows.

"Do you think I'd have come to you if I'd actually done it, and what's more would have told you?"

She shrugged her shoulders.

"You said you loved me," she murmured. "Why wouldn't you have come to me even if you'd actually…"

"You think I'm capable of such a thing?" he cried out.

She looked at him.

"I don't know," she finally mumbled, and her eyes assumed a look of uncertainty. "Or," she continued after a moment, "would you have rather not come to me if you'd done it?"

He was silent for a moment.

"What do you think I'd have done," she said, "if you'd come to me to say you had killed? Do you think I'd have screamed, woken up the house, reported you?"

"I wouldn't have come at all," he stammered.

"No?"

He was silent.

"I told you yesterday," she said, "that you don't really love me."

"Why not?"

She straightened up, went into the room and sat on the edge of the bed.

"Because otherwise," she said, and brushed her hair back, "you'd have had to come, even if you'd done it. If you loved me, you'd have had to tell me you had done it. If you were prepared to do such a thing, you should have believed I'd be prepared to listen to you."

There was silence. They looked at each other. Then he slowly went over to her.

As he advanced, she shrank back almost imperceptibly.

He was now no longer the man who'd spoken to her on the street because he'd fallen in love with her, and who could be dismissed because it would be too awkward to exchange more than a few words just because he happened to have a lovely pair of eyes. He was no longer the driver to whom one could say, "I don't need your car now. Please stop pestering me, especially in front of my house." He was no longer someone one wouldn't want to meet again because he was a nonentity from heaven knows where. He was now the one who'd be arrested the next day, and all her reserve, upbringing, status and sense of decorum crumbled into dust before the one who came to her, surrounded with the dreadful halo of crime. She had never imagined that she would actually listen to him, but now that he had come—in the middle of the night, agitated, harassed, pursued, lost—all her inhibitions vanished into thin air and she felt attracted to him.

He came close to her, drew her close and kissed her. Their lips merged. They sank back on the bed, and the darkness threw a veil over their closed eyelids, their fate, and their desperate love for each other.

# 10

H E WOKE AS THE GREY DAWN was creeping in through the curtainless windows. Marisabelle was still sleeping. He withdrew his left arm from under her without waking her. Then he got out of bed noiselessly. The windows looked out onto a garden. The early light revealed clumps of grey, denuded trees shrouded in mist against a background of damp tiles and dirty chimneys that appeared to protrude from a muddy sea of foam; the stark outlines of polished furniture, mirrors and fittings only emphasized the general gloom of the interior. Stretched out on the bed lay Marisabelle, her pale, mildly resplendent face framed by a mass of dishevelled hair.

It must have been about six o'clock.

He carefully groped around for his things and gathered them up. Then he tried to look Marisabelle in the face. In her sleep she had drawn her eyebrows together as if she were not sleeping at all, but reflecting on something anxiously, though for the rest her face showed that she was indeed asleep. Like all people in the land of Nod she looked remote and indifferent, as if she were dreaming of something intangible and short-lived that she would not recollect on waking.

He wanted to kiss her on the mouth, but decided not

to, in case he woke her. Anyway, what would he have said to her if she woke? That the morning had broken, and all was at an end? Everyday thousands of people get up and say, "Adieu, that's the end." There's no need for it. It's a complete platitude.

He bent over and brought his face close to hers until he could feel her breath. He waited a little, quite motionless. That was their last kiss. Then he left.

He closed the door silently behind him and crossed the entrance hall; the keys were still in the door to the apartment. He opened it, stepped out, and closed the door behind him.

The light was on in the staircase. He had walked down one flight when it suddenly went out. The pale dawn was already trickling in.

Down in the entrance hall the porter had just unlocked the front door, and it was he who had switched off the light. As Sponer approached, the man looked at him in amazement that he was still in the house. Sponer walked past, but suddenly turned round and said, "Is something the matter? Maybe you think I've stolen something? Why don't you report me to the police? Go on, report me. We'll go together. But just imagine what they'd say if you were to report me simply for spending the night here." Then his thoughts wandered back to Marisabelle again. He swung around and walked away. In the meantime he had resolved not to go to a police station, give himself up and expose himself to all the bureaucracy. Instead he decided he would return to the

Bristol, go up to Mortimer's room, call the police and await his arrest with a certain degree of dignity. He walked down Alleegasse and came to the municipal gardens where he had spoken to Marisabelle, disturbing, as he approached, a flock of crows which rose cawing from the lawn. Noisy, fast city traffic was at its peak. All the slow-moving carts from the country were gone.

A tram came rattling round a bend. He crossed the Ring and walked into the Bristol.

No one stopped him when he entered. Surprisingly, there weren't any porters in the lobby either. No one was standing by the lift, though a couple of staff came out of a side corridor and scurried up the stairs.

He followed them slowly. He turned left at the first floor. There was the shimmering marble corridor again, brightly lit, windowless, claustrophobic and hermetic, as in a dream. Or like the passageway between the cabins of a sunken liner, he thought. The lights were on because the electricity generator still hadn't stopped working. The water couldn't get to it. The compressed air kept it out. It's a wonder the floor wasn't sloping, he thought.

The air really felt as though it were actually under pressure, overheated by the central heating, dry and dusty as last night. He was breathing heavily. Farther on, he saw a group of people standing in front of a door, some entering, others leaving.

It was Mortimer's room.

Ah, he thought, of course! I quite forgot. The police are already here. No doubt going through Mortimer's luggage. Why though, if he's dead, as they must know by now, do they still want to rummage through his belongings? And then he remembered that he had locked the door when he fled, and the Montemayors had been left locked inside for some time; he couldn't help smiling at the thought.

He still had the key in his coat pocket. He'd hand it in before he was sent to prison, so the hotel wouldn't be the loser. No one, of course, would pay the bill.

However, he realized the Montemayors would have been able to ring the bell or phone for the doorman, and someone would have come and unlocked the door. How in fact did they get out?

He was wrong, they were still there.

When he reached the door, he glanced into the entrance hall and saw Winifred. There she is again! he thought. She was making a statement which was being recorded by several people who were standing about; some hotel staff were also present, though not the night staff, who had been relieved. It was now already day, though the light was still on in the entrance hall. The door to the salon was shut.

Winifred was still in her evening gown, her brocade coat slung over it. In her left hand, hanging down by her side, she held her handbag, and rested her right hand on her hip. Funny, the way she stands there like that, Sponer thought, erect as if giving a speech. She seemed really proud of the fact that she had exposed the false Mortimer. She could at least have changed her clothes instead of parading around in her red and gold finery. She was being questioned, and replied in the way that prominent people do when answering several interviewers at once; everything that she said was being taken down. However, the men stood there with their hats on, not even bothering to remove them in the presence of a lady.

Now, Sponer thought, how embarrassing! She's putting on airs, insisting on playing the prima donna, even though Montemayor may in the meantime have already woken a lawyer and started divorce proceedings. However, I'm number one here now.

He stepped into the hallway. Winifred looked up, while the others wrote down something she had said, and caught sight of Sponer. He could see from the expression in her eyes that she recognized him immediately, but surprisingly she ignored him as if he didn't exist. Instead of shouting out, "That's him!" she just looked at him for a couple of seconds and then turned away.

Sponer was, he had to admit, more than surprised. Had he simply imagined that she'd looked at him? But the others, too, ignored him completely. One of those taking notes, and another person who had just dictated the last statement verbatim in German, appeared to be from the police. And the others, Sponer wondered, who were also writing things down? Presumably reporters. There was also another man there, obviously someone from the hotel management to judge by his formal suit. The hotel staff stood there as if they were just doing their job, their hands by their sides, listening attentively to what was being said. They all looked at Winifred, and no one paid any attention to Sponer. One of the detectives was dictating, the others were writing, and the staff looked on.

He wanted to go up to them and say that here he was, that he'd come voluntarily, but a strange sense of unreality suddenly overcame him. None of the people bothered about him. It was also true that no one had bothered about Mortimer either when he lay dead in the car and the passersby hurried past as if nothing had happened. But they had looked for him, Sponer; Marie Fiala hadn't returned, she'd been detained... Or, he thought, maybe there was some other reason why she... What? It was conceivable, of course, that they still didn't know that I... But Winifred knew, of course! Why was she behaving as if he weren't there? He was overcome by the bizarre fancy that he actually wasn't there, that he'd simply imagined that he had checked in at the Bristol...

Just then, the detective who had been dictating asked Winifred another question.

"When," he asked in passable English, "did Montemayor leave you yesterday evening and when did he return?"

"He returned from the rehearsal at about five-thirty," Winifred said. "We had tea in the lounge, but he left after a few minutes and said that he still had to attend to something. He took the lift to his room, but came down after a short while. I was still sitting there and saw him come out of the lift, walk past the office and the porter, and then leave the hotel. He returned just before seven o'clock. I was already in my room…"

"From where you had already called the Bristol in the meantime?"

"Yes. I then heard my husband enter the salon and go to his room."

Every word was noted down. Sponer looked from one to the other. Winifred glanced at him again. She couldn't have failed to notice him this time! However, after a brief moment's reflection she glanced away. The detective asked her another question.

"When was it," he asked, "that you entered the Bristol?"

"About one o'clock in the morning," she said.

"And when did your husband come?"

"He came immediately after me."

"I mean when did he enter here?"

"A quarter of an hour, half an hour later; I can't remember that exactly anymore."

The detective continued his questioning while all this was being written down, "Did you know Mortimer was a gangster?"

"No," she answered.

"But your husband did."

"He said he did."

"And you? Did you think it was possible?"

She shrugged her shoulders. "Yes," she said. "It was possible. My husband said it was even common knowledge over there."

"How then do you explain the fact then that the police didn't take any action against him?"

"Against Mortimer?"

"Yes."

"Which police? The American?"

"Yes."

She laughed dismissively. "You don't understand, here," she said. "The police over there don't take any action against gangsters. Against a petty band of crooks, maybe. But certainly not against people of Mortimer's standing. The police are far too powerless for that. They can't afford to expose public prosecutors, senators and possibly even their own people who may be gangsters. Besides, at any time Mortimer could have come up with the excuse that he was being protected."

"How do you mean?"

"I mean he'd have claimed the gangs had put pressure on him and he had been obliged to do what he did. Protection means that business people, bankers and industrialists are left in peace as long as they give a certain proportion of their income to the gangs. Mortimer could simply have come up with the excuse that his own bank was under protection, and the police would have had to accept this since they were in no a position to shield him against such protection."

The detective gave a sign to indicate that these comments were off the record.

"So," he said, "Montemayor claimed, therefore, that Mortimer had been the victim of bandits?"

"Yes. These people are always fighting one another for control. It's a case of open gang warfare. Don't you know that? Doesn't it happen here?"

"No."

"Really?"

"Our police," the detective observed curtly, "appear to be more efficient than the American."

"Or your bandits," Winifred retorted, "appear to be less ruthless than theirs."

"We don't wish to go into that!"

Winifred shrugged her shoulders.

"All the same," she added, "my husband had a better opinion of your police than I have. Otherwise he wouldn't have wanted to prevent me reporting the crime. He assumed, however, that even if I'd reported the driver, it wouldn't have misled the police, and they'd have tracked down the real murderer all the same."

"No doubt," the detective said.

So, Sponer thought, the driver—that was him.

"Do you think so?" Winifred said. "Of course, as has already been said, José was also of the same opinion, though he still maintained for a long time that I'd only cover the tracks of the real murderer if I reported the driver, with the result that he'd never be found. He prevented me using the phone, and after the driver had gone, José kept on and on about it until almost morning, and only then did he give up."

The detective began translating this into German and dictating it. Sponer took this opportunity, stepped forward and touched the detective's arm.

"Could I have a word with you, please?" he said.

"Yes, what's the matter?" the detective asked.

"Here I am," Sponer said.

"Who are you?"

"I am Ferdinand Sponer."

"Oh?" the detective said.

"Yes. Ferdinand Sponer."

"And what do you want?"

"What do I want?"

"Yes. Were you told to come?"

"Told to come?"

"Yes, told to come!"

"No, I came of my own free will!"

"Then please be kind enough to wait," the detective said, "until you are called. Please don't interrupt the proceedings." And with that, he brushed past him and continued dictating.

Sponer, bewildered, stared at Winifred, but she ignored him completely. She opened her handbag and looked inside, then closed it again. The others just stood still and looked straight ahead. Sponer asked himself whether he was going mad.

"Montemayor," the detective continued, "wanted to leave with you this morning?"

"Yes," Winifred replied.

"After the driver had gone, your husband must have said to himself that both Mortimer's and the driver's disappearance would be noticed immediately. Didn't he want you to report the matter after all?"

"No," Winifred said. "He tried to silence me right up to the end. And it was only when he finally realized that I'd report the matter as soon as I could that he told me the truth. He even believed that the police, once they'd got the driver, would also be sure to find the murderer. I didn't agree. I thought that they'd suspect the driver and no one else. My husband would have denied everything he ever said to me and he would have talked himself out of it. That's why I shot him."

Sponer could have sworn he misheard her. Was she mad? Whom had she shot? Mortimer? Impossible! But the others, too, when it was now being dictated in German, appeared not to have understood, judging by their calm looks.

"Mortimer's Colt," Winifred continued, "was still lying on the table where the driver had left it, together with Mortimer's other things. Montemayor finally said to me that even if I didn't want to keep quiet, in spite of him begging and even ordering me to do so, I'd surely keep quiet after I found out that it was he, Montemayor, who did it because of his love for me. I didn't quite understand him at first. Then he said that he'd known when Mortimer was arriving, had driven to the station, waited until Mortimer had left the station and got into a taxi, whereupon he had jumped on the running board from the other side as the taxi drove off, opened the rear door, fired several shots at Mortimer, slammed the door shut, jumped off, run away, and was back in the hotel a little later. After he had finished, I took the Colt from the table and shot him."

The reporters went on writing. The others stared silently at Winifred. The words hit Sponer like an avalanche. The car screeched, Mortimer's car, with Montemayor on the running board, the shots echoed in his ears, the three bullets that had passed through Mortimer on that fatal journey... The dark night, the drive with the dead man on board, the streets, the surge of the river, the dark staircases, the look in Marisabelle's eyes, the greying dawn—the scenes of the night all raced through Sponer's brain like a terrible tornado.

"José did not love me," Winifred continued. "It was only vanity, jealousy and hatred that drove him to kill Mortimer. But I loved Mortimer with all my heart. If I could have died for his sake, I'd have gladly done so. Now he's really dead, and I'm alive. But my life is merely a sacrifice for him, because I killed Montemayor for his sake."

There was a pause. The detective said something in connection with the statement to the effect that it would still have to be corroborated by evidence that Montemayor had actually murdered Mortimer. The sequence of events leading up to the murder could, however, be provisionally reconstructed on the basis of the available evidence.

He opened the door to the salon. Montemayor lay there on the carpet in his evening suit and, with Winifred at the head, they all filed into the room and stood round the body in silence. By the light that poured in through the windows, the powder and rouge on her face looked strangely incongruous. Her bleached hair appeared unreal, and the folds of her crimson evening gown seemed to shoot up her body like tongues of flame every time she moved. Montemayor lay stretched out on his right side, his fists clenched, and his face, which was turned upwards, was already deathly white. At the same time, however, it bore a strangely calm and serene expression.

For even though an ocean separated this city and the savannas, he had fallen like the true peon that he was. He had fallen like a peon falls in a fight with his enemy, a fight for a beloved one, with a bullet, with Mortimer's bullet, in his heart.


While the rest stood there in silence, Sponer started backing away without making a sound. Nobody took any notice of him. Slowly walking backwards, he reached the door. Feeling behind him, he opened it, bounded out of the room, slammed the door and ran along the corridor, down the stairs, through the entrance hall and the revolving door and out into the street. He ran straight across the ring road. He knew that, come what may, he would still have to report to the police and make a statement, and would have to explain the disappearance of the body. But now, at that moment, he just couldn't be restrained. He ran across Karlsplatz, through the gardens, and down Alleegasse to Marisabelle's house, flung open the gate and dashed through the entrance hall and up the stairs. He stopped, breathless, in front of the Raschitzes' flat and rang the bell. Still panting for breath, he pulled his cap off his head and smoothed his hair. The door was opened after a short pause. The young girl to whom he had spoken the night before stood there. He wanted to say something, but was still so out of breath that at first he was unable to utter a word.

"The Fräulein!" he finally stammered.

She stared at him. "It's you? It's you again?"

"The Fräulein!" he repeated. "Please call her!"

She appeared not to understand fully.

"But she hasn't come home yet!" she finally said.

"Not home?"

"No. She isn't back yet. What do you want to see her for? Don't you know where she is? Has something happened? What is it you want from her?"

He was no longer paying any attention to her. Marisabelle must still be upstairs! He turned and ran up. The girl stared after him. At the Dorfmeisters' flat he rang the bell and banged on the door with his fists. He leant one hand against

197

the door and rested his head on it briefly, before quickly bringing both hands to his face and closing his eyes, and although he was still gasping for breath, he suddenly smiled; he smiled as if in a dream, as if it were once more Marisabelle's hands in which he had buried his face.

He heard light, hurried steps; he straightened up, and the door opened.

It was Marisabelle, woken from her sleep, her hair dishevelled, a fur coat slung over her shoulders. He stepped silently over the threshold, not taking his eyes off her, hands outstretched towards her.

She looked back at him in amazement.

"I…" he finally stammered, "I'm free! It was Montemayor."

She shrank back.

"What?" she stuttered. "Who?"

"Montemayor! The man who killed Mortimer… It was because of his wife… He told her he jumped on the car and shot him during the ride from the station."

She retreated a further couple of steps.

"Why are you here then?" she finally asked.

He didn't understand. "Why am I here?" he asked, and took a breath and tried to laugh as he looked at her.

"Yes, what made you come back?"

"Where?"

"Where? Here of course!"

"Where else?" he shouted. "Where should I return other than to you!"

"Keep your voice down!" she hissed. "You're mad! Go away!"

He didn't understand.

"Go away!" she repeated.

"You want me to leave?"

"Yes! Immediately!"

"I don't understand you," he said.

"I don't understand you either!" she shouted. "What on earth induced you to come running back here! What if someone sees you?"

He stared at her. He wanted to say something, but his lips didn't respond.

"Did you too think," he finally stammered, "that you wouldn't see me again?"

"Well, at any rate not now!"

"Ah," he stammered, "you only did it because you thought I'd be lost otherwise?"

"You're not anymore, though, are you?" she shouted. "You say that you've been released!"

"Is that any reason why I should go away?"

"Someone may see you! How could you leave without waking me? How could you let me go on sleeping upstairs here? You compromised me!"

"I compromised you?"

"Of course!"

"And in the night," he shouted, "I didn't compromise you?"

"In the night you were on the run!"

"In other words, you only did it because you thought I'd had it?"

"Do you hold that against me?"

"I don't, but why are you ruining everything?"

"You're doing it yourself! You're putting me in an impossible position!"

"That I should have thought of you before anyone else?"

"No, by coming here! What does that make me then?"

"The same what you were for me in the night!"

"So?" she shouted. "And what about you?"

"Me?"

"Yes. You're now free, you say! You're no longer what you were! And besides, it's no longer night now. What on earth did you mean by compromising me?"

"That's the last thing I wanted to do!" he stammered.

"Yet you're doing it now! And what's more, first you come to me and say you're lost, and now you come and tell me none of it is true and nothing has happened."

"I thought," he mumbled, "that you'd be happy for me."

"Of course," she said, "but nevertheless, how on earth can you put me in such a position?"

"What position?"

She didn't answer. They just looked at each other.

"What position?" he repeated. "You mean of seeing me again?"

She was silent.

"Are you trying to tell me I had no right to come back?"

"I'd have done anything for you, but you shouldn't have then turned around and told me that it wasn't necessary. It's all over now, and you shouldn't remind me of what I did. Don't you understand?"

So that's how it is, he thought. Understand? Oh yes, I do understand. At least I'm beginning to understand. There are women one shouldn't see again, and there are men who shouldn't make a nuisance of themselves. Drivers, for example, if they've had a fling with a girl from a posh family. There are girls that one shouldn't compromise, and others who'd gladly let themselves be arrested for a man. Those whom one shouldn't question about what they had been up to, and others who would have it splashed all over the papers that they wanted to sacrifice themselves for you. Girls to whom one mustn't return, and others who wait for years and to whom one doesn't return...

"Don't you see," she said, "you can't just turn up here like that? You're compromising me, you must show me some consideration! If I got carried away last night,"—she cast her eyes to the ground—"that was something else. But now you can't just barge in like that. You're forgetting that..." She broke off, searching for words.

"You're quite right," he said after a pause. "I'm forgetting that you're not some girl from the suburbs that I can see when and where I please. I'm forgetting that you've got to heed your reputation, otherwise your family will disown you. I'm forgetting that it's impossible for us to be seen together, that

201

everything that you did for me was just a one-night stand, just a matter of a few hours, and that you can't be my lover. I'm forgetting that I have to forget this. Nevertheless, I thank you," he said, and came close to her and kissed her hands. "I thank you for doing what you did."

With that, he looked at her for a moment, then let her hands fall and turned. She grabbed his arm. "Listen," she said, "I don't want you to think that I…"

She fell silent. There was the sound of someone coming up the stairs. They were quick, hurried steps, two treads at a time. The next moment Marisabelle's brother appeared in the doorway. He looked at them both, as if wanting to say something. However, when Sponer approached the door, he stepped back onto the landing.

Sponer crossed the threshold. At that moment the young Raschitz leapt from the side towards him. Sponer, as quick as a flash, turned round towards him and knocked him to the ground.

Then he walked away.

He walked slowly, his hands in his pockets, through the suburbs. In his eyes there was a strange expression, as if he didn't quite see where he was going.

After for some time, he lit a cigarette. After a couple of puffs, however, he noticed that it tasted of honey. He still had one of Mortimer's cigarettes. He threw it away. It was more than half an hour before he came to his district. However, he didn't turn off in the direction of his flat, but went to Fiala's house instead.

He walked past an organ-grinder standing in the pouring rain. His instrument was covered by a sheet. He was playing 'Castilliana'.

As he walked past, Sponer tossed him a coin, for the song stirred something in the depth of his soul. He had heard it before, only he no longer remembered when and where.

Then he saw Marie standing on a street corner.

For a moment he was overcome by a feeling of shame. But then he realized that he must overcome it.

When Marie noticed him, she came running towards him, almost tripping over in her excitement, and held out the envelope containing the money. Then, sobbing, she threw her arms around his neck.

He embraced her, and they stood there for a few moments without moving or speaking. A couple of people turned and glanced at them.

He stroked her hair.

"Thank you," he said, and took the money. "But I don't need it anymore. I'm not guilty."

"What did you do then?" she sobbed.

He kissed her. "You probably won't know what I'm talking about," he said. "I was just on my way to you. I was Jack Mortimer."

# Translator's Dedication

*For Karen*
*Verzeih! Forgive me! Прости!*

## Translator's Acknowledgements

My thanks go to Jane Shuttleworth, the Dostoevsky expert, who read my translation, and Gerlinde Buchberger, who read the novel in the original; both of whom offered many kind words of support and encouragement; also to John Francis Moloney.

Last but not least, I wish to acknowledge my gratitude to the highly efficient and helpful Pushkin Press editorial team headed by Gesche Ipsen and supported by Bryan Karetnyk, but above all to the Publisher Adam Freudenheim who was a helpful and wise presence throughout.

*The Pushkin Press Classics list brings you timeless storytelling by icons of literature. These titles represent the best of fiction and non-fiction, hand-picked from around the globe – from Russia to Japan, France to the Americas – boasting fresh selections, new translations and stylishly designed covers. Featuring some of the most widely acclaimed authors from across the ages, as well as compelling contemporary writers, these are the world's best stories – to be read and read again.*

## MURDER IN THE AGE OF ENLIGHTENMENT
RYŪNOSUKE AKUTAGAWA

## THE BEAUTIES
ANTON CHEKHOV

## LAND OF SMOKE
SARA GALLARDO

## THE SPECTRE OF ALEXANDER WOLF
GAITO GAZDANOV

## CLOUDS OVER PARIS
FELIX HARTLAUB

## THE UNHAPPINESS OF BEING A SINGLE MAN
FRANZ KAFKA